Dedicated to the everlasting memory of
Dian Wilson

Goodbye my Lover. Goodbye my Friend.

All is never lost... ɔu are n⸱ t... *still there*
is love..

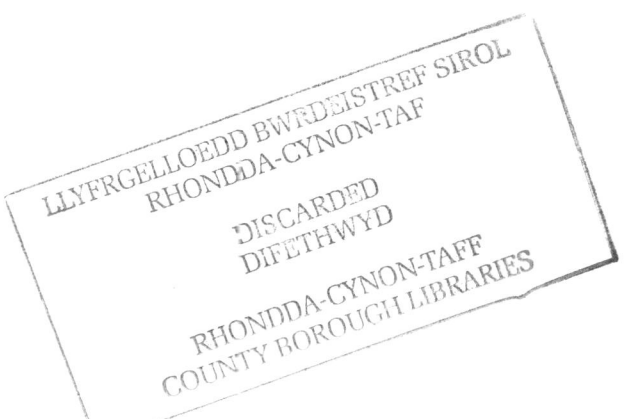
1

Proof Read by: Eileen Harries
Edited by: Grace Smith
Specialist Advice: Erica Harwood
Publisher: Artbully, UK

Goodbye my Lover. Goodbye my Friend.
A novel by Carys Smith

Prologue:

*I promised you a white horse if ever
  you began to forget.
You promised I would be the last
  to be forgotten.
It seems we both forgot to remember not to forget
  to remember our promise.*

  Zan

**Dian and Lyse
Before – 1995**

The green man faded into a mocking red. Lyse the shorter of the two, clung onto Dian's arm which was wrestling with the flimsy umbrella and fighting the violent gusts of wind- driven rain. For a long moment, they, and every other battered, hapless pedestrian, dodged the spewing mud splatters and waited resigned, for permission to cross.

"Tell me again why we are doing this" said Lyse, leaning in, half irritated, half grateful to the wicked weather for the opportunity to be so casually, so innocently close. "May I remind you that it's only October 25th not December, or even November."

Dian grinned down, blue eyes sparking pleasure with her sudden idea to buy a Christmas tree now. The best were only just in the shops. They could have their pick. Should they go for traditional green or the modern white? Would Lyse, even consider the purple? No. If her apartment had been on the ground floor she would have insisted on the inconvenient although beautiful, pine needle- dropping genuine article. Thank heavens then, for the third floor!

"But isn't this fun, sweetie?" Dian was happy. For once Christmas was not something to altogether dread. "We can have Christmas Day every day for the next two months. Well, for the next six weeks anyway before everything gets so busy for William and I have to go away and be a wife.

Lyse squeezed Dian's arm hurrying her across before the transient green image disappeared. As they toiled their way through the untidily peopled precinct, making for the arcade at the top end, a small silence grew between them. Their buoyant mood dipped a little as each became preoccupied with their own uneasy thoughts.

As soon as they reached the entrance their spirits gave an upward lift, their good humour completely restored as they exchanged a glance of bemused delight at the unexpected early bright trappings of a Christmas in full swing. The centre had gone big and early this year.

"You were right. This is going to be fun!" Lyse was immediately sucked in by the multi coloured energy of a thousand fairy lights and the magic of a gigantic tree whose star spangled top disappeared somewhere into the glass ceiling. She pushed off all those unwelcome thoughts around the wisdom of her choice. She hummed them away with Bing's "White Christmas" and sniffed appreciatively at the tempting wafts of cinnamon spices coming from the hot chocolate stand, grinned back at the gingerbread men and women displayed on red chequered table cloths along the centre aisle.

"Of course we can have a pretend Christmas," she conceded and considered the manikins prominent in the window of Ann Summers. They were dressed in not much more than a Santa hat and tinsel. Could she persuade Dian into such a festive outfit?

"Do I have to have a pretend present as well?"

"Of course not darlink!" Dian quickly smothered her dark introspections: the fragility of their unlikely romance: the stark reality of their weekday only life together.

"You can 'ave the preten' Christmas second to no. There will be many a present for you."

She easily fell into one of their favourite personas; lowered her voice and whispered in an exaggerated accent: sultry and suggestive; "*and* a very, very special one tonight if you would like it!"

***

Later inside the sweaty black cab Bing Crosby was rudely replaced by Meat Loaf, the festive smells by cheap air freshener and stale cigarette smoke. Yet their mood remained resolutely merry as they slid and slipped helplessly across the worn brown leather seat, hanging onto their boxes and bags taking turns quizzing each other with a bar from a well known carol.

"What would you like on our Christmas tree, apart from *this* little Christmas fairy of course?" Lyse broke off from their game, abruptly aware that she had no idea what to give this classy, sophisticated older woman who seemed to have everything already.

"I'd like to buy you something really nice. Jewellery perhaps, something you could keep forever and ever."

Dian shrugged, "Let me think about it darling girl," she peered through the steamy window at the crowded pavements and cheerful shop fronts for inspiration. She was secretly delighted with the extravagant romance of the question and found herself faintly blushing like a teenager. She and William hardly bothered with such things these days and when they did, it was always a predictable gift: something for his computer, another piece of antique glassware for her collection.

Vague remembrances of childhood Christmas shopping trips along these same little changed streets flittered across her mind. She and her father had never really known what her mother had wanted, had always had qualms when confronted with that phrase, "Oh, a surprise would be nice."

She caught a passing glimpse of his favourite statue – Jim Driscoll - working class boxing champion, and sighed. She would have to get something for Dad, not that he would know what the day was or what the giving of gifts meant. On one of their final walks together he had stumbled abstractedly past Jim lost in an incomprehensible conversation with an invisible companion. She would have to buy her own favourite perfume this year unless Lyse who loved the fragrance on her skin could accept that as a significant love token.

What if ... ? She pictured her own favourite urban statute - Aneurin Bevan. They had stopped briefly to admire it today. Instinctively she had reached up to touch the gold leafed inscription of her hero in just the same way Dad had always patted the bronze foot of Jim. *What if...*

Dian shivered the cab's over-heated atmosphere suddenly all pervasive and clammy. She turned to Lyse, picked up her hand and with an unusual lack of caution pressed it against her lips.

"Would you give me a promise for Christmas?" *I shouldn't ask it but ... what if ...?*

"Can I have a clue first?" Lyse, puzzled by the unexpected serious twist to their conversation scrutinized Dian's face, noticing the tired lines around her eyes, the tight, trembling line of her mouth. Had there been just a trace of over exuberance this afternoon – the way there often was after a recent visit to her father's care home?

"You're not asking me to promise to grow my hair are you?"

Dian rubbed a circle in the foggy glass with a ragged piece of tissue and looked back out onto the street as they jerked to a stop at a red light. *What if she did not recognise that familiar stained glass window in St John's Square for example; or ...* Dian's heart gave a panicky lurch. *... heaven forbid, the name of this much loved woman by her side?*

"What if I'm like my Dad? What if you noticed me start to forget things would you, could you...?" *This was stupid. It was unfair. But what if...what if... William would be no good, it would go against everything he believed.* Dian rushed on, before her common sense had time to reassert itself.

"Could you possibly promise to help me? Help me go somewhere before it was too late. To what is it - Dignity?"

"It's called Dignitas, I think." Lyse replied slowly, a coil of apprehension snaking through her stomach, "but that's just silly. You're not your Dad." She had never met a woman so entirely in control of her own world, so astute, so piercingly intelligent and entirely in possession of her own sense of self. But she did have a rich imaginative streak that sometimes made her a little too prone to tip over into morbid flights of fancy.

As the taxi finally lurched forward Lyse gripped at the glitzy, glittering bags of their first Christmas future together and determinedly reassured herself: Dian was still only in her mid-fifties. Morris was getting on, must be over eighty. Dementia was an old person's disease wasn't it? Anyway, could you inherit it? Impossible! Unimaginable!

"I promise." she said, "If that day ever comes but it won't, I'll magic that ridiculous old white horse up there on top of The Angel and," Lyse waved an airy arm at the hotel they were passing, "I'll fly you across the sea and sky for your own chosen time of oblivion. As long as you promise me that if you do forget, you'll forget that blasted Sir William first!

Part one

2012-2016

"Looking for what was lost... in the blink of her bright blue eye." White Tiger: Zan 2014

Chapter One:

Lyse and Dian

She was late: again. Lyse checked her watch then glanced up at the wall clock. Took the stairs two at a time and scrutinised the numerals of the Teas-made in the spare bedroom: her bedroom. All ready with a clean duvet set and a quick dust round. There were tea bags, sugar, a couple of digestives and a few mints. *Where is she?*

From the window she could see across the slate-red roof tops and up the hill as far as the main road. There were two vehicles coming down. One was a low white open sports car, the other, a shirtless teenager on a battered bicycle. *Where is she?*

Twenty five minutes late. Did that make it time to ring William? Lyse crossed to the extension and picked up the phone and then replaced it. No. She still hated speaking to him. Even after all these years, even though he was just plain old William now, Dian's shadowy figure of a husband. *Where is she?*

Still no sign from the road apart from Mrs Next Door's lime green Skoda, Darren walking his dog, school boys with skate boards. *Where is she?*

Lyse hurried back down the stairs and picked up the address book. Had she recorded the new number for the third mobile she had bought Dian this year? Yes: would Dian have left it like she had suggested in her jacket pocket, or lost it like the other two?

With rapid fingers she tapped in the number and waited. It rang. It cut off. She dialled once more. This time there was a rustling and static, a radio in the background; a click then silence. Hell. *Where is she?*

On the third try there was a far off tremulous voice.

"Hello, hello I'm here." A small laugh, "I'm somewhere anyway!. I'm losing myself again!"

"Are you driving?"

"No. I'm doing the other thing...the standing still thing."

"Dian, sweetheart," Lyse took a deep breath and kept the question calm, light.

"Can you tell me where you are?"

There was a long pause. Lyse heard the window go down and then outside noises; a distant laugh, door slams, chatter.

It sounded like a car park. Where though? *Where is she?*

"It's a big car place. Oh and an orange sign. It says... Sainsbury's. It's a Sainsbury's... somewhere."

Lyse could just make out a muted conversation begin and then the faltering exchange of the handset. Dian, courteous as ever "Excuse me..excuse me..where am I?"

"Hello?" the voice was deep, puzzled or embarrassed. It was probably a man then.

"Would you mind telling me where you are? My friend is lost I think. *Where is she?*"

Dian

Where am I? How did I... miss that... it ... again? Stay a minute, remember. That fog... clear soon. Comes and forget...goes and remember. I'll just wait. Late for... somewhere?

What's that ...speaking... no, talking. Ah, it's the radio. That's good. Thought for a moment... like Dad ... imaginary people! What's a ringing from that pocket... a phone thing in a pocket? Yes, a phone thing from... darling girl.

"Hello. Hello*" oh damn... the red button...green I want.* "Hello. Hello. I'm here. I'm somewhere anyway." *May as well laugh.* " I'm losing myself again!"

Lyse and Dian

Lyse and Dian sat close together on the small sofa. Although the mid June evening was warm there was an unspoken comfort in their shared body heat and their familiar scent: Dian's perfume, Lyse's soap and shampoo.

Lyse shuddered at the memory of the rush and the fear she had experienced on the frantic drive to the supermarket. The excruciating, heart rending first sight of the dear, but uncertain face looking down from the long plate glass of the upstairs cafe. That helpless child like wave, the apologetic excuses. That was not her Dian - could not be her Dian.

Yet it was and that was when they should have sat down and tried to talk about it. They should have bought a drink and delayed the "follow me home" drive back and then the desultory chit chat about how confusing the new bypass was, what to eat and the turning on of the television.

Dian's thoughts were busy piecing together her sentences. After today she could not put it off any longer. She would have to explain about the fog that inexplicably came down, the way it drifted across her mind in waves, shrouding every thought and intention in a thick impenetrable cloud before quickly clearing like a sun-filled sky after rain.

Did she still have command of enough language to describe that terrifying temporary loss of self? Or the way that self somehow seemed just a little more diminished each time it finally returned?

Every day it comes every day it went...no..goes. What happens if it comes and stays and never wents. No. Goes – goes –goes! What happens then?

"You know kid how scatty I've been lately?" Dian drew out her intractable words, willing them into the open space between them. Only her hands betrayed her anxiety as they twisted her rings and brushed down her bracelet.

"You know I've always lost things, lost my way, turned up late, all of that..."

"I'm sorry I was grumpy." Lyse pictured the ungracious way she had stomped out of the cafe. Her heart lurched with shame with a sudden conscious sense of a precious moment already lost.

"We should have had a look round the shop. We could have got something better for tea. *Had* a cup of tea! It's that new bypass."

Lyse knew she was evading, delaying, searching desperately for other explanations, other reasons.
"Why don't we both buy one of those sat nav. thingies? I'm as bad as you at finding my way round this new road layout. We're both getting too old for change."

She ignored that faint insistent flutter of fear beneath her ribs, hid behind a desperate wisecrack,

"Well, you are anyway!"

"No love." Dian half turned on the sofa and took her hands, seeking those dark blue darting reluctant eyes, fixing them with her own.

"This is not like before. I need you to listen to me. While I can still ... explain... say everything I need to tell you..."

"No! It's nothing like that!" Lyse felt her mind shrink and squeezed her eyes shut, "You aren't your Dad. It's not that. It can't be. I won't...won't hear you say it!"

Always hard hates hear anything un ... un ... bad too many times to try drops into ...always into ... what is that word... deny mode? No, denial, denial: too late for that now.

There was a small silence. Dian determinedly hung onto the sudden clarity of her thoughts; the blessed but definitely temporary, reassertion of her language.

Finally Lyse forced herself to look up and meet the light blue of those familiar loving eyes. She saw sadness, acceptance and glimpsed a faint, cloudy uncertainty at the corners.

"You already know and I already know so just let's say the words." Dian gave an apologetic shrug,

"I'm so very sorry darling girl, but it's Alzheimer's disease and somehow I have it."

For a heartbeat Lyse forgot to breath. Any possible reply strangled itself in her throat. There were too many thoughts rushing in at her. They jostled and jockeyed for position leaving her silenced until she eventually forced out one vehement sentence,

"Don't apologise. You don't have to apologise. You must never apologise to anyone. Ever."

Chapter Two:

Lyse and Dian

Lyse stood uncertainly on her front step watching the small red car until it rounded the bend and was out of sight. For a fraction she hesitated and then dashed upstairs reaching the front bedroom window just in time to catch sight of its steady progress to the top of the hill. It stopped at the traffic lights. It waited at the red and then made the turn onto the main road. At least she had indicated and turned left. At least she was going in the right direction: for now.

Dian had insisted on driving home, had forbidden her to follow and adamantly refused to ring William. She had seemed so much like the recognisable Dian, the confident, no nonsense, totally in control Dian. Lyse had meekly acquiesced. It was only once the battered Honda had vanished that all her doubts flooded back.

That other Dian was still there lurking behind this morning's cool confidence: The Dian of yesterday evening. The one who had waved anxiously down from the supermarket cafe like a small child lost. The one that apologised for having an awful, unspeakable disease: the Dian who had assured her that,

"Even when I forget your name and forget it I shall, it will only be my mind. My heart will always remember. It will never forget *you* my sweet, sweet love."

Later, Dian had suggested that they make love, even though it had been the longest time since they had shared a bed.

"Whilst I still remember how...darlink!"

They had laughed and joked their way upstairs and somehow had easily found and fumbled their way back to the intensity of their earliest romantic days. Lyse looked across at the unmade bed and wondered when or why that side of their life had drifted away. What had been that something or someone....?

From long habit, Lyse abruptly shut down that thought and began to tidy the sheets, reluctant to change them. The musky odour of Dian's perfume lingered, bringing back a vivid picture of the passion and the warmth they had so unexpectedly shared. Dian's glasses and her book of crosswords lay open face down on the bedside table. Those forgotten glasses again!

That was nothing new but even Lyse, who never enjoyed cross word puzzles, had always impatiently found them incomprehensible, could see from a glance, that most letters, although neatly squared across or down, did not relate to any known word.

She stood flicking over the pages, painfully working through the evidence. Months earlier each puzzle had been lucid and exact, last month a little less so and now, just a jumble of nonsensical letters. She hastily brushed away the tears that stung and pricked at the back of her lids and grabbed at the extension and pressed in the number.

Her hand shook, her mouth went dry. She did not want to talk to William. He would not want to talk to her. She had seen the dislike in his eyes when they had briefly met at Morris's funeral. She disliked him too or at least she had, once. This though could not be about her or William. It had to be about Dian and only Dian.

When the ring tone switched to answer phone Lyse thankfully dropped the handset. Instantly she picked it up again and this time when the message request clicked in she left one in a tone as steady and as matter of fact as she could manage.

"Dian lost her way yesterday. She is on her way home. It's 9.30. There is a mobile in her pocket. The number is......"

Chapter Three:

Dian and William
The diagnosis

Dian delayed leaving the Ladies cubicle. That waiting room was just too much: the irritating canned music; the sporadic coughing from across the way, William's stoic silence. There seemed to be an overpowering smell of antiseptic in the air that made her eyes water.

Nasty at the nose that one. This music new ...different?

There was something about the clinic today that was unfamiliar. There was a dense claustrophobic atmosphere setting her nerves on edge. The small print in the magazine had made her queasy, each word bleaching into the next. She had given up trying to read and made an excuse to escape to the toilet.

She turned to the splash-streaked mirror to check her lipstick. For an instant she did not recognise the woman who stared bleakly back. The reflection swam and distorted under the inadequate lighting.

Where was her face? Whose face might this be?

There was a light insistent tap at the door. It was William. Her number had come up. It was time. Dian smothered a frantic desire to run screaming from the building. Instead she straightened flushed the toilet a second time and plastered a grim resolute smile on her lips. She gave a little wave at the glass. Reassuringly, the image waved back.

At least I'm still me.

She opened the door to follow William into the consulting room. It was time.

***

There was an eerie, exultant moment just after the diagnosis when Dian experienced a great weight fall away followed by a rush of inexplicable, indignant, justified relief. She had stood, almost before the consultant had finished speaking, her customary charming politeness markedly absent.

"Thank you." She had said briskly, holding out her hand as if to shake his dismissal," Well, that's better...better now you know what I know. Perhaps we can do some..." she searched for the word," help."

She thrust the appointment cards and information sheets at William and almost danced out, her eyes glittering in triumph.

Tests and tests more tests ... have said now. I knew all at once...no...long before...too clever they said...too many points...I know...knew...knew! Those that's gaga not I... me...never do listen...but..."

Dian waltzed through the exit and into the car park. As she paused, unsure which car was theirs, a cold chill wind of shock cut through her satisfaction.

I have it. Alzheimer's disease. Dad's disease. Now nothing can do...

When the consultant began to deliver the diagnosis William had automatically rearranged his facial features to settle into the same benign pose he usually reserved for encounters with his most difficult of clients. He successfully maintained this facade even as Dian had sprung from her seat, thrusting the leaflets into his startled hands, leaving him to make all the arrangements for a follow up appointment with the memory clinic.

The motorway traffic was fast and free flowing. For once it was an easy drive and demanded far less attention than he usually gave this stretch of road leading into the city. Consequently, he found there was too much uncomfortable thinking time. His mind dragged him back to the sight of this clever, sometimes too quick witted and erudite woman, struggling to correctly place simple numbers in sequence or failing the picture test of a watch from a clock. He recalled the way a faint tinge of embarrassment had coloured her cheeks as she puzzled over the simple line drawings: the way she had twisted the rings on her left hand every time an answer eluded her.

Dian checked once more for her purse and asked, for the third time, "Where are we going?"

William squashed an unwelcome flash of irritation, "I'm dropping you off to meet Erica for lunch at The Tea Shop."

"Oh that's good," she said again, "I could just do with a nice cup of tea."

He gave a furtive sideways glance at his wife of over forty years sitting so unusually quiet, abstractedly fidgeting with her handbag. A passing glimpse of his face in the rear view mirror revealed that the polite mask of earlier seemed to have set solid.

He wondered with a faint stirring of unease whether this was the face he would have to show to Dian and the rest of the world from now on. He wondered also how it would change this semi-separated life of theirs.

Was this the heavy price he would have to pay to get his wife back?

Chapter Four:

Erica and Dian

Erica bang on time as usual was already at their favourite table in the corner. It was fairly secluded but situated with a good view of the door if you were waiting for a late-arrival as she invariably was. Today though, Dian was well past her customary fifteen minutes.

Still, that no longer mattered now she was retired. Erica complacently opened the menu and searched for their all time favourite – Portuguese tartlets. She and Dian had been meeting here for well over twenty years. Although the name and decor had changed numerous times, astonishingly the tartlets always remained on the menu and always tasted just as delicious!

Unfortunately the gilt edged mirror was the same too, placed inconveniently opposite, giving her ample time to consider how her once slightly greying hair was now almost white. Were her features beginning to resemble her mother and grandmother just a little too much for comfort?

As the over long arrow hand of the former rail station clock clicked onto the hour Erica grew uneasy. It was already two o'clock. Last week Dian had forgotten their lunch date completely. She had waited half an hour then called and re-arranged for today. Had she forgotten again or what could have delayed her this time?

After ten more minutes Erica searched under the table for her bag, deciding she should check for a missed text. She looked up a little irritated at the new door alert, the tone was down-right silly - a knock instead of the usual bell chime! Her face cleared as she saw her friend hurrying towards her. Close behind though, was a tall, bulky man with a slight stoop and a receding hairline. Was that William? Was he joining them? Erica's heart sank, the man was almost impossible to talk to!

"Bonjour, ma cherie" Dian said brightly, leaning across and air kissing Erica's cheeks, "Pardonney moi d'etre en retard."

Erica was unaccountably relieved to find Dian in such high spirits. She deftly replied in the same vein, more than happy to continue their jokey imperfect French exchange, "Ca n'a pas d'importance ma cherie!"

"This is William," Dian said, suddenly looking a little blank, lapsing back into English. She gestured vaguely at the man behind her, "Have you met before?"

"Of course we have – quite a few times." Erica gave a polite smile and glanced at William, "are you staying for lunch?"

William shook his head and gave a short, incomprehensible chuckle, before pulling out a chair for his wife. Erica watched perplexed, as he took Dian's elbow, only letting go once she was safely into her seat. She had never taken him for the solicitous type of husband.

"I'll be back in an hour and a half then?" he said hovering indecisively, awkwardly patting Dian' shoulder. For the briefest second he caught Erica's eye and inclined his head towards Dian who was busy reading the menu as if oblivious to his continued presence.

"I'll be back at three thirty."

This... list a mess. Words running all over like ... spilt milk. No... ink! New glasses or different fog?

Dian dropped the menu onto the table and met Erica's enquiring look with a vague smile, "I can't decide. Shall we have what we always have*?"*

What do we ...well, it doesn't matter. I'll have to ... do it.

***

William arrived promptly at three thirty and bustled Dian away with merely a nod, leaving Erica to gaze after them helplessly, feeling as if she had not been given time enough to say goodbye: as if she had already lost her friend. Why couldn't the man have just sat down for a few minutes? Helped them make another arrangement or done the sensible thing and allowed them all to discuss his wife's, her best friend's bombshell? Well, they were obviously not "all in this together!"

Was it such a bombshell? Had she really not noticed until today? Absently she picked at imaginary specks on her skirt. How many late arrivals or missed appointments had there been? How many sudden awkward pauses in conversations where Dian had seemed to lose the thread? How many weeks, how many months had she been brushing aside what must have been blindingly apparent if only she had wanted to see it?

Erica tussled with the unimaginable thought. They would probably never meet here again to enjoy their Portuguese tartlets. To gossip, confide, plot, laugh and yes, just occasionally, disagree.

She surveyed her friend's half eaten meal and the barely sipped tea. Was it all lost then? Lost in the blink of an eye with Dian's casual announcement, made just as William reached their table, leaving her no time for a response?

"I had the tests today. Didn't I tell you? No, probably not...." Dian had leaned confidentially across the table and with a stage whisper and a phoney French accent had added, "You see ma cherie... I'm prone to a bit of forgetting. It is my Pere's Alzheimer's."

Erica continued to sit on, long into the afternoon with coffee she let grow cold and struggled with the idea of finding a way to grieve for the loss of a person who still lived.

Finally as she threw the change onto a saucer for the waitress her thoughts turned to Lyse. She and Dian had once sat at this very table and, rather successfully, as it turned out, discussed how to rescue Lyse from herself and...

Erica deliberately suppressed any further unproductive historic remembrances of over a decade ago. It was the here and now that mattered. One thing was certain. Dian, like last time, would expect her to help Lyse.

Erica gave a heavy sigh and picked up her bag. Somehow, she and Lyse would have to work together to bridge that almost insurmountable barrier called William. If not, Dian would be completely lost to them.

***

Dian and Erica
Dian's lost memory - 1991

Dian drew up to the parking space bordered by imposing yellow lines and a white sign tied to the railings stating in proud capitals: "PRINCIPAL." She applied her hand-break and let the engine idle, her front wheels just touching, but not quite crossing the fresh paintwork.

This was a promotion she had not expected or had particularly wanted. With only the merest hint of tact, her chief had made it clear that it was either this or an early retirement package along with dozens of her less fortunate colleagues.

"Really Dian," he had hardly dared meet her eye, "we can't think of anyone more suitable than you. You'll be a new broom, a breath of fresh air, a..."

"Yes, thank you Derek," Dian had cut in smoothly, deciding that fifty four was just a little too young for retirement, but far too old to be flattered. "I'll take the appointment of course."

She sat for a while and studied the outside of the old sandstone edifice with its tall blackened Victorian chimney stacks, the roof that had far too many missing slates and the dispirited peeling paintwork.

She watched as the students jostled their way through the narrow back door, hurrying towards their first class of the day. Cheerful greetings in at least a dozen foreign languages drifted across the grass and through her open window. It was easy to pick out French and perhaps Spanish and German but...

Finally she shook off a hopeless longing for her former work day haunt with its cosy double glazing and automatic PVC doorways, the helpful ramps in place of steps, the familiar friendly reception staff and her comfortable community timetable. Time to suck it up kid!

Resigned she released the brake and allowed her car to creep forward into the designated square and finally switched off the ignition. Tilting the rear view mirror forward she rummaged through her cluttered handbag until she found her lipstick, mascara and a brush. War paint was needed, and if even half of what she had heard was true, plenty of it!

***

Erica Remembers
1991

There was no real need for Erica to tidy up the notices but it was better than feeling like a spare part as she waited in the foyer to greet their new Principal. As she prised the drawing pins out of the much used and worn cork board she threw a quick glance up at the clock. Nine fifteen. Mrs Williams was late for her first day and Erica was now late for her first appointment. She, Erica, was never late.

Determinedly she quashed an unworthy dart of smug self congratulation and any further peevish thoughts about being overlooked for the vacancy: yet again. That was hardly the fault of Dian Williams and she had vowed to greet her with an open mind, if not quite an open heart.

She patted her jacket pocket and felt the reassuring bulge of the enormous collection of keys she had planned to present with a welcoming flourish, fifteen minutes earlier. They rested awkwardly against her hip, dangerously insecure in the gaping cavity. Erica sighed and left her half finished task and began to make her way to reception to leave them with Jenny or Rose. Mrs Williams would just have to ask for them and show *herself* round. She, at least, had work to do.

"Hello! Hello! You must be Erica Harwood!" the cheerful greeting unexpectedly came from the front entrance, where the swing doors had been rudely thrust open and now were painfully creaking themselves shut.

Erica hurriedly rearranged her face into a polite enquiring mask and took a moment to register the identity of the visitor. Was it possible that this slim, almost slight figure in that elegant blue silk dress with the carefully made up fine features was Mrs Williams?

As if reading her thoughts Dian grinned impishly and ran a hand through the streak of silver in her dark well brushed hair, "Oh my dear! Yes it's me, the new girl is late I'm afraid!"

Erica gave a bemused, smile, startled to find her proffered handshake brushed aside and replaced by an extravagant air kissing of both cheeks which was followed by a murmured, "Excusez moi. Je suls en retard."

Not to be out done Erica gave a quick, instinctive response, "Tu es pardonnee mon enfant."

Their eyes met in mutual amusement. Erica dug out the keys and handed them over with far better grace than she had envisaged she would feel only a short while earlier.

"Welcome, Mrs Williams, Dian. Here are the keys to our kingdom...your kingdom I should say."

Dian charmingly accepted the unwieldy bunch with a mock little bow and then tossed them negligently into her crowded handbag.

"Thank you ever so, but first things first, where do you keep the kettle?"

Chapter Five:

Lyse and Margaret
2012

Lyse was at the front desk in reception, giving Jenny a chance to acquaint Hazel, the new recruit, with their rabbit warren of an old house turned school building. She could hear the echo of their footsteps on wood as they trudged up the three flights. It was good to have found someone who could do the running for them. How many times in a day did one of them have to make that upward journey? How had they all grown so old together without noticing? Rose had retired two years earlier and she was now part time. Jenny was sure to be next.

She pictured her much younger self, wildly racing her students up those steep steps and with a sharp poignancy, the way her charismatic and utterly charming new boss Dian Wilson, had poked her head round this same office door shaking her finger in mock reproof.

Through the open French windows Lyse could see clear across the grassy seating area to the cluttered car park beyond. She easily picked out her blue Nissan, once again carelessly parked under the ancient Acer now splendid in its mid-summer, dark crimsoned leaf.

It was a lovely day. Above the tops of the houses beyond, she caught glimpses of an almost cloud free blue sky and a high dazzling sun. This room, with its stone walls and high ceilings was always a little chilly, even on the warmest days. It was a shame to be inside and for a moment she was tempted to take the afternoon off.

She had a sudden almost desperate urge to see her mother: To hide behind one of her afternoon teas and bright chat about the garden and hilarious tales of the local Ladies that Lunch club. Over sixty and still running to Mum! What was she like - as the kids would say!

Instead, she picked up the phone and calmly suggested she drop in on Friday afternoon. Margaret, pleased, promised to rustle up one of those teas. Lyse joked that the crusts needed to be cut off and the sandwiches made into triangles. Margaret, caught up with the spirit of things, offered to bring out the best china and Grandma's embroidered tablecloth.

As Lyse replaced the handset she wondered whether she had imagined that her mother's antenna had immediately tuned to alert mode just because she had offered to visit out of turn. Was that an intuitive offer of comfort food? Or had Dian reached C in her address book already? Had she begun to carry out her plan to make a farewell call to each of her friends?

If Dian had already telephoned surely Mum would have said something? The two had been friends a long time, enjoying epic shopping trips that often slipped late into the afternoon. Those had dropped off lately though. When had they last gone out together? Three months or surely not, six?

***

***

Margaret went into the kitchen to ransack the cupboards for the makings of a proper old fashioned tea cake. The currants would need to soak for a couple of hours. The tablecloth could do with a press. It was nice to have a tea to plan, a cake to bake. There hardly ever seemed any point of going to all that trouble just for one.

She shook out the fruit, seeping it in water before carefully folding in the flour and adding the eggs and butter. As she sorted through the cake tins, searched for the glace cherries and hunted for her mother's old recipe book she continued to speculate on the reason for this unexpected visit. If Lyse wanted no crusts and triangles something was amiss.

Her mind ranged over the possibilities. Once it would almost certainly have been something with one of the children or an argument with her sisters. These days Lyse seemed to have opted for a quieter more solitary life. Her world firmly centred on a few chosen old friends, her work and her gardens. Those inexplicable couple of disastrous romances seemed to be safe in the long distant past.

Margaret carefully creamed the mixture in the way she had been taught years before, using the same china bowl and the exact wooden spoon. These old hands of hers, with their arthritic joints and age spots now so closely resembled her mother's that she could almost imagine them standing together at the table conjuring up the famous fruit cake into being.

How often had *she* run home for tea and sympathy? Was that invisible umbilical cord never truly severed?

"Mothers were born to worry, even when there is nothing to worry about" Grandma Beatrice Olive had often said when she had offered up the plate of crust-less triangle-cut sandwiches with a slice of her homely, comforting fruit cake.

Perhaps it was nothing. Margaret batted away her concerns and went to find the tablecloth. As she passed through the hall she gave a small twitch of surprise as the telephone gave its startling shrill cry. Twice in one day!

After a long period of static and almost silence, eventually a voice distant and yet familiar hesitantly asked,

"Is that Margaret...yes... that's it... Margaret Connor? This is... Dian. I'm ringing you to call goodbye...no... calling to say goodbye."

"It's lovely to hear from you Dian! Are you going on holiday with..." Margaret trailed off a little embarrassed. Was it with William or Lyse? Is that why Lyse was coming down, to discuss a holiday?

As Dian began her explanation she listened with growing alarm through half sentences and longer and longer pauses as her friend searched for a word, a phrase: the point. Finally, with a sinking heart, she was certain she had heard correctly: a diagnosis and Alzheimer's disease.

Margaret forced herself to wait patiently through the muddled explanation as it continued to tumble across the line. Absently she twisted, tied and untied the telephone cord until finally Dian lost track or had run out of words.

"Are you sure?" Margaret quickly corrected herself, "Of course you are. This is really hard for me to take in. I'm so very glad you have told me yourself but..." she rushed on, worried in case Dian hung up or her own emotions became too obvious.

"I don't think we need to say our goodbyes just yet my dear...no, not just yet. You're always telling me "So many shops, so little time!" Well, we had just better get on with it. Write me in for Thursday. I'll pick you up."

Margaret continued her cake preparations with a much heavier heart and the sad conviction that until she could think of anything more constructive for Lyse, the traditional consoling tea party would have to do.

Yet, there must be more she could give.... and not just to Lyse but to Dian whose certain loss from her own life she hardly dare contemplate, let alone from her daughter's.

Chapter Six:

Lyse and Dian

The flash of bright red sleeve continually glimpsed from the corner of her eye was disconcerting. Lyse put more gentle pressure on the brake, slowing down to an almost crawl. It was tricky. The downward curve of the road was more of a hair-pin bend and the other drivers were losing patience.

This was another new thing. The hanging onto the grab handle above her seat and now a flinch accompanied by a loud shriek as the car that had tail-gated them for sometime flew by almost clipping their wing mirror. Having Dian in the car was getting to be dangerous. Lyse surreptitiously checked she had clicked on the child locks and counted the minutes before they reached the cinema.

Once inside there was the inevitable hesitation at the bottom as they searched the packed rows of bodies for two seats together. The dull blue gleam from the aisle lights hardly made an impact as they began to carefully negotiate the half dozen steps cast in treacherous ambiguous shadow.

Lyse felt the sudden warmth of Dian's hand as it slipped into her own when they began to squeeze their way through feet and knees towards the remaining two middle seats.

"Will my bag be lost?" Diane asked for the second time.

Feet and knees...feet and knees...bag...my bag...

"No!" Lyse guiltily recognised the note of irritation in her reply." It's fine love. I'll take care of your bag, as soon as we sit down."

A brief flash of brightness from the screen illuminated their chairs and Lyse thankfully pulled down Dian's, hastily grabbing the bag before the question would be asked again.

"Will my bag be lost?" Dian began a frantic, noisy, search beneath her seat.

Feet and knees..dark and feet and knees..bag...my bag

"My bag...is left... somewhere...the car?"

In spite of the semi-darkness Lyse was all too aware of the covert looks they were receiving. She experienced a fleeting, unreasonable rush of anger towards all those uncomprehending strangers. She took a deep breath and reminded herself of how often they had indulged in loud sighs and stage whispered complaints at noisy late comers; had ostentatiously shifted away from the intruding wafts of over salted butter popcorn, had groaned loudly at the sound of hands that rustled and groped around in sticky cartons.

She sat down quickly and placed the bag on Dian's knees, looping the strap through her own fingers.

"The film's going to start now." She handed over the glasses from her pocket, "You had better put these on if you want to see anything!"

"Thank you, lovely girl. I'm being Mrs Bumble today." Dian included the crowded row of occupants into her apology, treating them to one of her new self-effacing smiles. She pushed on the spectacles and settled herself, slipping a couple of jelly beans across to Lyse from the bag she always kept in her pocket.

Lyse felt her throat catch and the familiar smart of unshed tears. How could this be? Her one time lover and even longer closest of friends, had, by that simple action of passing a few sweets, been miraculously returned to her if only for a blessed moment as if she was not irreversibly vanishing with every meeting, with every outing, with every phone call.

***

Lyse Remembers

When Lyse arrived Dian was already there, casually lounging against the corner of the kiosk in a long green padded jacket with deep pockets, a jaunty red scarf at her neck and one hand still in a black leather glove that matched the expensive looking handbag slung negligently across her shoulder.

She looked so elegant, so deliciously attractive. Lyse stumbled to an abrupt halt. Dian always put her clothes together so well, and with that sweep of grey white hair...

Lyse had completely forgotten about the close press of people coming into the foyer behind her. She looked across at Dian whilst making her apologies and realised that her discomfort had not gone unnoticed. One wry eyebrow was raised, the bright blue eyes amused.

"I'm sorry. I'm late." Lyse tried to suppress the strange tingle in her fingertips. She had an absurd desire to lift that leather clad hand to her lips. Instead she opted for an awkward peck on the cheek, "You know what work is like."

"I've almost forgotten what the word work means my dear." Dian took her arm and slipped it through her own, "Now, do let's hurry in and get cosy. I've already got our goodies." Dian patted one of the deep pockets, "You don't eat that awful smelly popcorn do you? If you do we'll have to sit three seats behind each other!"

Lyse shook her fringe from her eyes in almost truthful denial. All thoughts of a small box of toffee popcorn evaporated as they hurried past the sweet counter and into the cinema. Her head swam a little at the suggestion of getting cosy together in the warm stuffy dark.

All day she had imagined this moment. The conveniently placed middle row seats they would effortlessly slide into, the already purchased gift of chocolates she would present with a gallant bow, the mildly flirtatious conversation in between the advertisements and trailers.

And now here she was, craning her neck and dithering at the foot of the ill-lit steps: late and with not even a *bar* of chocolate. She could see nothing but a pyramid of packed rows of faceless people already pulling off coats and tearing open sweet packets or shuffling through the suddenly despised popcorn.

"Come on, I can just see two together up there with the gods "said Dian, taking her hand and pulling out a miniature torch. She skipped them up the gloomy aisle to the back row and made short work of the awkward side steps across feet and knees.

"You're a real pro." Lyse whispered impressed as they eventually settled themselves just before the credits appeared. Dian's apologetic wisecracks and charming sharp white toothed smiles had smoothed away all the annoyances until only good will had followed them into their seats, "You've turned arriving late into an art form!"

Dian grinned and pushed her glasses up the bridge of her nose before reaching into her other pocket and slipping across a handful of jelly beans.

"Of course, darlink! I haf done this many a time! I am the origin girl- scout! Alway be prepar..ed!"

Lyse swallowed a snort of surprised laughter, immediately recognising the complacent self assurance and the flawed English of a mutual colleague. "You're awful!"

"Yes, darlink...." Dian pressed her arm and leaned a little closer until their shoulders just rested together, "...but you like me, I theenk!"

Throughout the film Lyse could not resist an occasional furtive glance at her companion. Their shoulders remained just touching, the gloved hand lying temptingly on the arm rest between them. Oh what a plank she was! How had she ever had the nerve to ask this clever, supremely confident and sophisticated woman to come out with her?

What was this? Was this some kind of a date? A date! She had no right to ask anyone out for a date, and certainly not someone like Dian.

Lyse and Dian

For most of the night Lyse had remained sleepless and anxious, her bedroom door open. The keys were safely in her top drawer, but still she kept jerking into alert wakefulness, her overwrought fears manufacturing the distinct sound of a door slam or a car engine starting up. Isn't that what Dian had once told her that Morris had done - drove off into the darkness undiscovered until hours later outside his old home in his dressing gown— outraged that "strangers" were in his house?

The difficulties of their journey to and from the cinema still loomed large from her night- fevered thoughts as did the hurried retreat half way through the film once Dian's distraught keening had insinuated itself into her consciousness.

"No darling, it was just acting, just a film." She had carefully handed Dian the plastic cup of tea wrapped in a tissue, had stemmed hot tears with the corner of her handkerchief, determinedly ignored the curious looks from passersby, and repeated, time and time again, "honestly, it was just a film, just actors...yes I know they looked real, yes they did..I know they did..." until Dian had calmed down and had quietly begun to count out jelly beans into her lap.

Lyse began to lay the table. She shook in two unappetising ovals of Weetabix into Dian's special cereal bowl, added one sugar, just hot water, no milk. She poured the pale weak tea into the matching tea cup. Even after all these years she found it hard to believe that this was what anyone actually enjoyed for breakfast: found it impossible to accept the taste could be improved by the quality of a cereal bowl or a hand painted tea cup.

Another painful shaft of love and loss pierced at her heart. There had been so many breakfasts, so many films, so much love and laughter, so many tears and silly arguments. How could it all end like this? What did yesterday and now this morning mean for the remnants of their increasingly tenuous relationship?

Obviously trips to the cinema were no longer possible and today's tactful call from Frieda's taxi's, would mean that there would probably be no more overnight stays. If she was afraid to put Dian into her car was it any wonder that not even a lucrative weekly fare would be enough for any cab company to take the risk?

Lyse sank down into her chair, an overwhelming surge of anger leaving her unsteady on her feet. Lack of sleep was making her feel nauseous, weak and hopeless. Why had Dian stuck to that useless marriage of hers and why should she have to let her go? Why did it have to be today? She just wasn't ready. Damn Alzheimer's and damn that impenetrable wall called William!

Aware of tentative footsteps descending the stairs Lyse fiercely rubbed at her gritty eye lids and forced her lips into a smile. Dian stood, diffident and hesitant in the doorway, her blouse miss-buttoned, collar tucked into the neck, the back of her hair un-brushed and wearing pyjama trousers.

"My clothes are wrong aren't they?" she said with a hopeless shrug, beginning to undo her buttons, **"these just got away from me again, and ... and I lost my legs ... so I'm here like this..."** she flapped her hands, her voice trailed off into a small, embarrassed, girlish giggle.

Clothes all wrong...feet and knees...cars...apes not real...darling girl...scared...me scared... the fog does it. Got to...must talk... to say...

Dian continued to stand on the threshold, toying with her blouse, fishing for any fleeting fragments of memory or words that made sense. Lyse sat helpless, her smile slipping, searching desperately for a response. A silence stretched between them until Dian's expression suddenly cleared.

"You know something kid? This Alzheimer's a bugger. It's not just my clothes is it? I did something bad yesterday...in the car ... in the film, didn't I?" she stated, in her old familiar direct way.

"Yes it's a bugger alright, but it's not you that's bad! It's that disease. It's a stinking shitty monster!" Lyse burst out, "and it's a nice blouse even if you've done it up wrong!"

Their eyes met across the breakfast things, Dian lifted an eyebrow in that ironic amused way Lyse had always found so attractive and gave a lopsided smile. Lyse, feeling a weight lift, a shadow shift said,

"Tell you what. Let's go back upstairs and sort out your clothes. Then I think we should cook ourselves a real breakfast for a change."

"That's a wish...yes...but..."

To ding...no dong...no dial...what is it...oh what is it!

"Must ding dong dial whatever to..." who is ...who...the man...to say later..." she trailed off, the fog creeping back as she began to lose her precious thread once more.

Lyse was momentarily thrown before a dim light began to dawn. There was a new language here. An Alzheimer's Speak she was going to have to master. She sifted through the words searching for their meaning and grinned, suddenly triumphant,

"I'll ding dong dial the number!" she said," We can tell William you'll be home tomorrow after lunch."

Dian grinned back, *"Yes that's the man and tomorrow is lunch and maybe who...Mum...Margaret?"*

"What a good idea! I'll ask my Mum to come to lunch and she can sit in the back of the car with you whilst I drive you home."

"Ding, dong what!" Dian said pleased, beginning to snigger uncontrollably.

"Yep, ding dong whatever!" Lyse repeated, jumping up and joining in with yelps of relieved laughter.

She went to Dian. She hugged her close, holding on for a long, long, moment as they continued to laugh through their tears with a renewed conviction that all was not lost, that somehow they were still in this together.

Chapter Seven:

Ruby and William

When the door swung open and William came through, stooping slightly under the low framed door, Ruby hurriedly sidestepped into the Ladies and dragged a comb through her tangled grey hair.

An unwelcome picture of Dian in a flamboyant yet tasteful dress with her silver- white expensive haircut materialised suddenly to mock her own reflection. She twisted her ill-fitting skirt straight and pulled down the clashing cardigan. There was an unsightly stain that had gone unnoticed until now on her shirt collar.

Still, William would not notice. He never seemed to notice what anyone looked like...which was just as well.

Her heart sank as she inspected the hall. No one had bothered to clear up after Sunday's Bingo Blitz. There were too many tables, the chairs untidily thrown backwards, balls of paper and pencil shards still littered the floor. It had taken the best part of an hour just to coax the boiler into life and to fill the urn.

As she opened the cleaning cupboard looking for the wide broom she caught sight of the dog eared poster stuck on the inside of the door. Someone had circled the line:

> For the ungrateful
> We have done so much
> for so long...

It was probably Dian who had put it there. She had always turned everything into a joke, even other people's thoughtless neglect.

Well, it was true that William didn't seem to care whether The Cabin was heated or tidy either but that was because his thoughts were always elsewhere, especially these days: poor William.

Ruby unobtrusively pushed the broom through the tables, straightening the chairs as she swept, taking quick shy glances at William in his unassuming grey suit and his dangling huge hands as they sorted through a sheaf of papers. Finally he looked up and across with melancholy brown eyes and murmured, with an unfocussed smile,

"Hello, Mrs erm Mrs Winters. Thank you for coming in early."

"Glad to help, and it's Ruby, you'd best call me Ruby." She was uncomfortably aware of a faint flush beginning to stain her cheeks, "Now I'm on the committee. I think you can call me Ruby don't you?" she briskly swept the pile into a corner and out of sight and continued boldly, "I'd like to put cleaning rotas on the agenda for tonight, if I may?"

William jerked up his head in surprise. So it was Mrs Winters, Ruby, who had been co-opted onto the committee. He took in her cosily plump figure and her faded earnest hazel eyes and experienced a small swell of relief. Here was someone helpful for a change. Someone who was really interested and perhaps someone he could rely on?"

"Yes ah Ruby. What a good idea, I'll write that in now and," he paused giving one of his incomprehensible chuckles, "It's William, of course. William."

***

William
(two weeks later)

The moment William closed the door behind him there was a definite lift in his spirits. His shoulders loosened and he found he could straighten to his full height. He carefully made his way down the three steep steps towards the car noting that even his lame leg seemed to drag a little less with each one.

He switched on the ignition, indicated left but paused to look back at the new front door. He took in the two solid panels, unbroken by a window, the brass double lock and the matching heavy knocker and was satisfied. That was a safe door, no one was going to get in ... or out easily.

Unexpectedly the door re-opened. One of the cleaners was frantically waving. Ann or was it the other one, Annie, who hurried down to the car, closely followed by Dian. He sighed, rolled down his window a fraction and let the engine idle.

"Mr. Wilson you've not left us a key to the new door." Ann quickly took hold of Dian's sleeve before she could step into the road adding, "We need a key in case we go out with Dian, I mean Mrs Wilson."

William smothered a quick flash of irritation and schooled his expression into one of vague incomprehension.

"Go out?"

"Yes, to the shops...or the cafe, we always do, when the weather is nice, like today."

There was an expectant hiatus as Ann lifted her hand to receive a key. William's remained resolutely on the steering wheel and the open crack of window unmoving.

"I don't think so-ah- Ann. Last time Dian gave you the slip and went into the Co-op by herself."

"She was alright Mr. Wilson." Ann's reply held an indignant protest, "She didn't give us the slip! She knows the Co-op and we were right behind her."
William gave up trying to hide his annoyance. He was already late. He had been looking forward to Ruby's

consoling conversation and the cup of tea and sandwich she had promised he would be able to eat in peace and quiet.

"I think you and-ah- Annie should just come in and clean from now on," he said with a brusque finality. He pulled away pretending not to have heard his wife's halting protest or Ann's frown of consternation as she gently began to persuade Dian back into the house.

He started down the hill that led onto the main road giving a quick glance in his rear view mirror breathing a sigh of relief. The front door was safely closed and Dian was safely behind it.

Whenever he went out he needed to know she would stay safe and inside. There could be no more open doors and disappearing wives. There would be no more random keys given out this time, or any left lying around for Dian to squirrel into her pockets or handbag.

He was entitled to a little bit of worry-free time. It was the best decision for both of them.

***

Dian

Dian stood in the narrow hallway, half way between the living room and the kitchen, carefully examining the new front door. She took a few tentative steps forward and felt for the lock. The wood beneath her finger tips was now solid and smooth.

Where is ... turning thing ... the ...key ... up high now ... too ...too high for my ... no ... me

Her hands explored the unfamiliar metal basket that now enclosed the letter box. For a moment she fiddled with the catch but found it was beyond her. She took a step back, tilted her head, and studied the incomprehensible barrier that had inexplicably appeared this morning. She sniffed at the stale air, registered the reduction of light, the loss of traffic noise and people talk from outside and wandered into the living room.

Sun is now ... time to walk out ... no turning things ... dark wood blocks me... these bars a prison makes...

She knelt on the sofa and stared hungrily up at the sky and across at the houses opposite. She waved at the old lady with the pretty dog passing by. Dian wondered where her Dad had gone and then remembered. Dian began to cry.

When Annie came out from the kitchen she found Dian back in the hallway carefully examining the new front door.

Chapter Eight:

Erica and Lyse
(months later)

Her extension rang for the third time in an hour. Lyse sighed and considered leaving it for Hazel or Jenny before bowing to the inevitable. Her gruff greeting was met with a warm, amused and well known voice.

"It's Erica, Lyse. Erica Harwood."

Lyse, pleased by this unexpected distraction said, "Oh Erica, how did you ever cope with all this bureaucratic nonsense?"

She pictured her former boss as they had sat facing each other from across their desks for countless years. Erica's greying head often bent over a file, methodically and contentedly dealing with an over full in-tray, glasses perched on the end of her nose or more likely, buried beneath the paper mountain at her elbow.

"Well, I did warn you that you wouldn't like the job." Erica smiled into the phone, "I did suggest you might be more suited to the chalk-face!"

"Yes, you did and so did Dian. I've only got myself to blame." Lyse glanced through the grimy and barred window where a small patch of grass and her favourite bench still basked in the late afternoon sun. Erica's laugh must be what the laugh of a retired free woman sounds like.

There was a short pause and a slight clearing of the throat which Lyse instantly recognised as the one Erica always unconsciously used whenever she planned to broach any tricky subject: Dian.

"It's Dian I've called about Lyse." Erica said cautiously. "Have you seen much of her lately?"

Lyse closed her eyes and winced as a painful guilt swept through her.

"Not so much," Lyse rushed her reply aware that she was regurgitating all her mind's well rehearsed excuses. "Well not since we had to abandon the taxi visits...I just couldn't manage her in the car. Lyse clung desperately onto her last shred of self-justification, "she got so upset it was plain dangerous and..."

An uncomfortable vision of the way she had cowered behind the steering wheel when they had dropped Dian off surfaced. She had abdicated all responsibility to her mother, had left her to deal with the difficulties of communicating with the surly and monosyllabic William. She had momentarily felt only relief as they had driven away. Of course she had not meant to let three months slip by without even a telephone call.

"I just can't bring myself to arrange anything Erica." Lyse brushed away a stray tear, "I just can't make myself call that ... that ... I know he's her husband but I can't ask his permission to see Dian...as if he...he owns her!"

"Oh my dear Lyse! Yes, that's how you must feel of course. But Dian will never be anyone's possession." Erica's reply was sympathetic yet determined, "If you want to see her and she wants to see you, and I know she does, you must!"

In the brief silence that followed Lyse processed that thought.

She imagined Erica calmly smoothing her skirt over her knees, picking at imagined specks, prepared to wait indefinitely, wanting to offer whatever solution she already had in mind.

There had never been any point in evading Erica's iron will. "Could we go together, do you think?"

"What a good idea. I was hoping you would say that," relieved Erica forced her tone to sound brisk and cheerful. "I'll make all the arrangements and give you a call back."

The older woman replaced the phone, smoothed her skirt over her knees and stared through the wide bay window, searching for the calming solace of the newly formed early summer leaves that were at last beginning to cover the formerly winter-stark bare branches of their handsome silver birch.

It **was** hard to go there alone. Her intervention had not been entirely altruistic after all. She relived her last visit and the excruciating struggle to hold onto a coherent conversation with Dian for even a few minutes. It was much more than hard to witness her best friend's loss of self. It was harder still to realise that Dian was not completely oblivious to that loss and was fighting but failing with every day that passed. Every visit would be increasingly harder. The only outcome was heartbreak for them all.

***

Cheered by their conversation and Erica's promise to make the tricky call to William Lyse decided to leave early and drive straight to the gym. Miraculously all that crippling paralysis had been plucked from her shoulders by, of all people, Erica.

As she hunted for the bag neglected in her boot for weeks a half remembered long ago episode slowly crawled from the far reaches of her long term memory. Erica had held out another helping hand once before, which if taken sooner would have lifted similar feelings of guilt and anxiety that had hung just as heavy around her heart.

Then there had been an enervating reluctance to speak up. A piercing shame and self-reproach that had evaporated almost as soon as she was pressed into accepting help rather than continue to hide behind a stubborn painful silence.

Lyse shoved aside those vague disconcerting recollections and hurried across the crowded car park and in through the double doors. There was a new spring to her step and a burgeoning sense of purpose. For once she had no need to remind herself that she had told everyone that she had signed up for the half marathon. That she had taken their pledges and was going to look pretty silly if she failed to reach the finish line.

In the changing room she took out the tabard that she had hardly glanced at since the Alzheimer's Society had sent it to her. She shook the creases from the blue and green strip experiencing a surprising, if small, swell of pride and resolution. She could do this. If Dian had no idea what she was running for she would tell her anyway and show her the pictures and hopefully, the medal at the end.

Feeling a little self conscious she crept into the weights room which was full of uncomfortably long wall mirrors and bright overhead lighting. One or two other people were there working hard, looking enviously slim and fit in Lycra with labels and logos wearing special sport socks and fancy trainers with bright laces.

She examined the daunting equipment and unfolded the training plan Joe had written out for her. With a slow step she made her way to an oblong box with Reebok writ large on its flat top. It looked the easiest. If she could do that one then she could do the next.

How hard could it be? Just one step at a time, one foot in front of the other. Not as hard as having Alzheimer's disease: not half as heroic as her precious Dian.

***

Fresh from the shower Lyse caught herself humming a refrain from one of the brash and ear splitting tracks that had greeted her in every new exercise room. What was it? It was something ironic about coming along and fucking up someone's life? Was that word really *fuck* surely not? No funk up- whatever that might mean: obviously a euphemism.

She dressed hurriedly, trying not to catch glimpses of her naked self in the tell-tale dressing table mirror, preferring to study the wooden framed photograph of Dian taken during one of their many holidays. There was an artisan chocolatier sign just visible behind the nonchalantly posed figure who had somehow managed to appear confidently elegant in faded-green sweat pants and a well washed elbow length T-shirt. This must be from their first magical and romantic Parisian weekend where Dian had impressed all day with her apparently faultless French and had made love to her all night whispering, "mon amour mon amour," and "ma douce fille."

She examined the picture minutely, lost in all its detail; the sweep of silver white hair, the wry lift of an eyebrow, the bright light blue of laughing, seductive eyes. Why had she found it so difficult to look at this lately? When had she begun to flinch away from the sight of that beautiful portrait of Dian, still whole: still sound in body and mind? Without warning, like a desperate thirst she experienced an impatient urge to drink in each and every photograph she had ever taken of Dian.

Yet as she blundered around the house a dim realisation took hold. There were no other photographs of Dian anywhere. But she had taken so many, especially in their early years together and way before convenient mobile phones with face book and selfies.

She had always taken that old pre-war Brownie box camera with them. It had belonged to her grandfather. The negatives had been absurdly expensive to have processed but had been worth it for their clarity of line and colour. So where was it and where were they?

There were plenty of others on display. Dozens were pinned up and down the landing walls or filling the mantelpieces and window sills. The children in various stages of growth, weddings, new born baby grandchildren, Grace with Ruby Red Dog and the cat family, landscapes, beaches and seascapes, students and colleagues on the back steps of their building yet nothing of Dian.

A cold shaft of doubt suddenly struck. How would dwelling on all those, for the most part, happy years together, as lovers and then friends, help? The here and now needed her complete attention. Get on with the training and start visiting Dian. This Dian needed her. It was best to try and leave the other one behind, for now.

Chapter Nine:

Lyse and Erica
(a week later)

Was that distant figure Erica in her familiar red quilted jacket after all? This familiar looking woman was standing by a very unfamiliar and completely unexpected blue car. Erica had driven that old, safe grey Ford for almost as long as they had known each other. Lyse squinted, tempted to put on her glasses. Surely a light blue mini cooper sports with a racy black stripe could not belong to Erica? Unconvinced she was going in the right direction she took a few slow steps forward. One red quilted arm waved impatient as the other flung open the door and threw a carrier bag onto the back seat.

"Well, well! So is this yours or have you borrowed it from one of your grandsons?" Lyse said, not bothering to hide her amusement.

Erica gave the roof a proprietary pat and smiled a thin smug smile, "I just fancied a change." She gave a quick, meaningful glance at her watch," Let's get going."

Lyse walked round to the passenger side and looked warily down into the bucket seat before gingerly climbing in, wishing she had offered to drive.

"I've printed out the route," she said pulling a scrap of paper from her pocket, "I'll navigate shall I?"

"Don't worry about that." Erica briskly started the engine and pressed a button on the dash board. A small screen lit up, displaying a perfect map with distinctive blue and orange road markings. It was accompanied by a disembodied voice with a cut glass accent giving the stern instruction to: "Turn left and then right."

"Meet Janet," said Erica with another small, complacent smile.

Lyse was quiet. A vivid recall of Dian at the huge upstairs supermarket window flashed through her mind. The little girl lost look; the idea of a sat nav. as an answer to their problem quickly aborted, the taxi journeys abandoned, leaving them this visit as the only option.

Never a good passenger, Lyse gazed out of the window at the ugly urban sprawl hurtling by, trying not to wince whenever Erica pulled up just a little too sharply. As the miniature car on the bold orange inched further towards their destination Lyse smothered an almost uncontrollable urge to rip the screen from its carefully positioned mount. Instead she forced out a few leaden words in reply to Erica's cheerful enquiries about old colleagues and swallowed down the nauseous panic that continually rose at the back of her throat.

Once they had exited away from the fast moving traffic Erica breathed an inward sigh of relief and bravely navigated the tricky narrow roads until they found the plummeting hill down to Dian and William's home and stopped outside, hiking up the handbrake to its highest ratchet before switching off.

"Well," she said, "shall we just go for it this time, play it by ear?" If only it was that easy!

Lyse nodded oddly reassured as she watched Erica absently brushing down the knees of her slacks, reminding her of all their shared difficult meetings in the past. At least she had Erica and her dogged diplomacy in her corner.

Erica pocketed her key and glanced across at the bay window of number 20. A familiar face was pressed against the pane and a hand was waving with an excited and heart wrenching childlike gesture. Her heart sank a little as she glimpsed the tall shadow of William turning away with a shrug.

As they climbed the steep steps Lyse noticed only the substantial dark mahogany door, vaguely reminiscent of a castle bailey without the small sentry towers at each end. Dian loved light and air, how she must hate this — all that was missing was a damn drawbridge.

She shuddered at the grating sound of a heavy bolt being drawn and the fumbling double turn of a lock. She heard the blood rush in her ears and felt again that old irrational jealous hatred of the man waiting to greet them – the gate keeper: Sir.

As Dian frantically pushed past her husband and stumbled down to welcome them Lyse hesitated to reach out; completely overwhelmed with the incongruity of their situation: the impossibility of a rapprochement between herself and the man that had always seemed as immovable as that bloody ugly door was now.

Erica put a guiding hand under her elbow and gently propelled her forward, saying brightly,

"Why don't you and Dian find her coat so we can have lunch at the cafe? Will you help me carry our presents in from the car William?"

***

Dian

Dian looks through the window. ***Persons ... people ...I know these***. She rushes from the room, her footsteps close on the heels of the man...***William...yes that man.***

She allows the younger woman to help her into her coat. ***I do know this one... this special one...her name...no can't remember.***

The outside feels big and loud. The floor uneven... ***tall houses move....rush of cars***... but the outside air is nice. She sniffs greedily and looks up into the ***blue*** and at the ***yellow***. She grips an arm of each friend...searches for a name...*a fleeting memory picture comes ...laughter in a downstairs place and...and love...love in a room with the one with yellow in her hair*.

"Lyse!" she says triumphant and studies the older one with... *the white "I do know you...I do...and I like you very much...but..."* she turns back to Lyse, *"but I love you!"*

Dian knows this food place. She grins her best sharp toothed grin at the tall thin man with the tail on his head..."*your..*" she brushes at his soup stained apron..."*needs a new ...a new look."*

Charlie laughs and clears her usual table. He wipes the plastic clean and pulls out her chair.

"Here you go, Mrs Wilson." he says. There is only kindness and respect in his eyes. Dian reads this and her smile widens *"Yes yes a new one and the food?"*

Dian stares down at her dish: *Red on plate I like*
She pushes aside the bacon: *But animal is not mine.*

She considers the cutlery: *This four prong I know*
Moves it across the table: *The spear I now forget it*

She picks up a chip: *So my finger eats.*

Erica and Lyse exchange an anguished look, both are frozen into momentary silence, their minds and hearts grappling with the enormity of the change; the downward spiral in just a few months; the unendurable loss they are witnessing.

Dian takes Lyse's hand and holds it tight under the table.

"Mrs Bumble today," she says slowly. *"I used to be clever once,"* with a sympathetic look at her friends she adds, *"don't worry about it and I won't!"*

End of Part One

Part Two

2016-2018

..”black clouds pulled across...blue and yellow gone...
Haiku Zan

Chapter One:

William

William stood irresolute between the living room door and the hallway. Where was best? Was it better to see them arrive through the window or listen for them coming up the garden path? They were late. Any later and there would be no time for anything but book keeping.

He looked across at Dian who was now peacefully dozing on the sofa, clutching a woollen brown and cream knitted dog against her chest, a check blanket made from the same material covering her knees. They were half way through May but she had complained of the cold until he had reluctantly turned on the heating and then plugged in the coal effect fire just to stop her insistent:

"Flame! Flame! Flame!"

An immense sadness swept through him as he tried to recognise this prematurely ageing woman as Dian; her emaciated figure in the grubby mismatch of clothes, the lank hair she refused to have washed. This creature; rather awful to behold; bore no resemblance to the glamorous and well heeled woman he had always been proud to call his wife: had always wanted to keep as his wife regardless of what or rather whom, had continually taken her attention from him.

Abruptly he turned his gaze to the window, surprising himself with a furious rush of angry bitterness that only intensified his frustration at having to wait. For a moment he stepped back forty years and saw again his parents' faces as he had joyfully told them of his intended marriage – the quick glance of consternation that had passed between them. He recalled the words "a bit flighty for you my boy," from his father and the carefully guarded congratulations from his mother.

His father had been right of course and his mother's concerns justified. Had she ever really wanted him? She could have at least had the decency to leave him years ago. He had never been the kind of man to walk out on a marriage and well, only a complete and utter bastard would even think of it now. Oh, but he did think of it: often.

Finally! He hurried to the door and worked hard at trying to slide the bolt and turn the key with the minimum of noise. If Dian woke she would start that keening and try and follow him onto the street. Why today of all days had she decided he was her father? Yesterday he had been the old man lodger who lived upstairs. Out of the two he preferred the latter. At least then she did not dog his footsteps from room to room.

He stepped aside letting the two women in with a graceless acknowledgement and grabbed his things, hastening down the steps as fast as his lame leg would allow. Those women! If only he could do without them. For some unknown reason he was sure they found him deficient. There was always a cool disapproval behind their polite smiles, an unuttered inference that he was not quite the loving husband they thought he should be. A fleeting reminder of those two other women stabbed at his thoughts: that Erica and that Lyse. Lyse, whom Dian still greeted with overt affection, repeating and repeating:

"Darling girl! Darling girl!"

She was probably *that* woman. William jerked open the car door which connected sharply with the lamp post adding to the dents and scrapes already visible. Uncomfortably aware he was still being watched from the top step he pulled away, forgetting to indicate. A hooded cyclist swerved spitting out his cigarette, hurling obscenities over his shoulder. He saw Ann and Anna, or was it Annie, share a look and swore under his breath.

His hand blindly searched the passenger seat for the music Ruby had given him. He pressed the compact disc into the player and smiled. How had she known this was his favourite? Immediately the tightness in his jaw began to ease, his shoulders lightened, the knots in his neck loosened. He checked the dashboard clock. He was not as late as he had thought.

The frustrations of the morning slowly evaporated. His pulse eventually slowed to the even tempo of the music. How good it was to have a friendly face to look forward to. What he needed was a bit of normality after the morning he had endured.

As he pulled up and saw Ruby already waiting with her quiet patience he thrust aside any remaining guilty reservations. He would ask her. Would she agree to leave the accounts for another day? They could go for a walk along the seafront perhaps. Or have an afternoon tea in the park.

There was no harm in a walk together, or a quiet cup of tea and a piece of cake. They were only friends after all.

Chapter Two:

Lyse and Cassie

Lyse was taken to a corner table with a trellis that supported a very lifelike vine whose glossy leaves climbed all the way up to the ceiling. Settling into her chair she gave one of the plump purple grapes a discreet squeeze. It was a fake. Of course it was a fake, but a very good fake.

Her text alert pinged:

SORRY! SORRY! SORRY! ON WAY. 15 MINS. ORDER ANTIPASTO FOR TWO AND A GLASS OF MERLOT. A LARGE GLASS!!!

Cassie must have been locked on capitals for at least the last eight months. Her messages always gave the impression of a life lived at continual breakneck speed, as if the world was too much with her, or that everyone else was being left behind.

A pleasant looking waitress in a long ochre apron that swept her ankles came across, pen and pad in hand. As she returned to the kitchen Lyse was presented with an attractive rear view of an extremely short black skirt and

75

a pair of long bare legs, feet shod in very sensible shoes. Oh to be that young and that brave!

She gave the menu just a cursory glance. Cassie always ordered for them. Lyse knew next to nothing about food and cared even less. The decor was more important. This place had a cosy atmosphere with just a faint waft of background light opera. The green, white and red tricolour cotton cloth was set neatly with highly polished cutlery and wine glasses that glinted cleanly in the half light. The tables were evenly spaced for private conversation. Was she going to tell Cassie about the box she had finally taken down from the loft and what she was doing in her spare time at the library?

When their drinks arrived she sipped at her lemon and no ice tonic water, speculating about the large glass of Merlot. Cassie was most likely on a train then. Should she offer her a lift home? If so she would not get in until after ten. Lyse sighed at her own mean-spiritedness. Since when had she decided that her social life had to end at nine o'clock, or earlier if she could decently manage it? It was only the temptation of a couple of hours of frantic conversation with Cassie that had got her out tonight.

Her thoughts fragmented into long ago evenings with Dian. There had been so many late night cinemas and even later night bars, music and passionate love making, poetry in bed and cups of tea, long holidays and weekend breaks. Cassie was the same age as Dian was at the time of her diagnosis. She still seemed full of energy and lived life to the full. Was it continuing to work that kept her looking so youthful and vibrant and fashionably chic? That was how Dian should have looked but her mid sixties had been stolen by that wretched disease. It was hard not to resent everyone else their good fortune, even the glorious Cassie.

She pushed aside the ever present temptation to lapse into a circle of dark pointless rage and waved a greeting to Cassie who, as she hurried up the steps to the seating area, half tripped. Her bag went airborne, her cycle helmet rolling to a stop at their table.

Lyse bent down to pick up the helmet, handing it to Cassie who kicked it under the chair along with her bag.

"Don't let me forget them," she said and not quite seated picked up the wine glass and took a long hard gulp adding, "I like your hair that short and you've let it go grey well white really, it suits you." Her own hair was newly highlighted and cut into a stylish ear length bob, the pale green of her shirt complimenting the sea green of her eyes.

"You don't look so shabby yourself Cass."

The two paused and exchanged a look of frank mutual appreciation. Cassie wondered vaguely why they had never got together. Lyse squashed the unwelcome memory of an afternoon years earlier when Cassie had casually dismissed gender exclusive relationships as restricting "one's options for finding love." Is that all it had taken for her to retreat back into her cloistered, solitary world?

As her friend polished off one glass and ordered another, racing through her descriptions of an annoying colleague and impossible deadlines Lyse nodded along in bemused silence, waiting for her to run out of steam. She foraged through her mind for some amusing tale of her own that might divert Cassie away from the stress filled preoccupations of work.

"Do you remember that last time we met I told you I'd been asked to join the allotment committee?" she said when Cassie had finally talked herself to a stand- still adding with a ghost of a smug smile," Well I did."

"Oh do tell," Cassie said her interest immediately peaked. She picked up a bread stick and bit into it with a quizzical lift of an eyebrow, "Was my prophecy accurate. Did you find that behind those pretty rows of prize marrows they were harbouring awful prehistoric views?"

Lyse laughed out loud, encouraged that Cassie had actually remembered and impressed by her perceptive description.   Just like Dian, she had that way of lightening the dashing of a delusion; of shrinking it to its proper dimensions.

"Let's say that on a scale of one to ten of awfulness they would be about nine and a half!"

"An Elysium where only the great and good grow fruit and vegetables is a disturbing falsehood brought about by the likes of Monty Don. "Cassie said sagely, years of community ventures behind her. "I'm all ears. Tell me about your baptism of fire."

The Committee meeting

Lyse left the final two tomato plants in their plugs and reluctantly hurried from the quiet comfort of her greenhouse towards the Stores. It was an unpleasant May morning, the wind hard and strong for the time of year, carrying with it splinters of rain that spitefully whipped at the back of her neck. Not for the first time she regretted agreeing to join the committee. It was definitely not her kind of thing but she had decided it might help as a distraction away from the relentless decline of Dian and the ongoing difficulties with the brooding and sullen William.

In the two or three minutes it had taken to walk the length of the lane a howling gale had materialised from the sharp wind of earlier. A lone man was struggling to extract a huge deadbolt from a metal frame whilst three others huddled together in the opening of a nearby shed shifted their feet impatiently and threw the odd derisory comment in his direction.

She recognised the stooped figure. He always wore the same checked shirt and blue overall seemingly only held together by manure and mud. For a moment she dithered, tempted to disappear into the toilet block and leave the miserable old codger to struggle. He always walked off as she passed his plot, probably to save himself the bother of responding to her greetings.

"Hurry up man!" the one she had christened "Smiler" yelled and flicked his cigarette butt onto the tarmac. Lyse gave it an ostentatious stamp as she passed and hurried across to help hold the rattling iron sheeting. Finally Leonard Prosser ripped out the bolt with a grunt and shoved the door up half way before ducking inside with no more than a curt nod.

Lyse followed him in and quickly chose a chair furthest from the draft-ridden entrance. As the others took their seats she had a good look at them and at the building. She had forgotten how inhospitable the place was: how grubby and disorganised. She inhaled. Chicken pellets and what else? Jeyes Fluid? How unkempt and smelly the men appeared in this gloomy confined space. She edged her chair a little further back and pasted on a pinched polite smile, telling herself they had, after all, invited her to join them. It was not their fault if loud, large and rowdy men always aggravated and intimidated her in equal measure.

A big brawny man with thinning hair and a T-shirt pulled tight across an expanding waistline said something incomprehensible resulting in a cheer from the others. Even Leonard's face lifted a little and "Smiler" grinned from ear to ear. Plastic cups were handed round and a generous helping of Glenfiddich was sloshed into each one.

"Go on Kilt," said Smiler, "offer the lady some. She's one of the boys now!"

"No she's not," Wilfred Jones said pushing past Smiler and handing Lyse a dog eared exercise book and a thin ballpoint pen, "She's the Minutes Secretary and she's got to keep a clear head or we still won't have any minutes taken.

There was a muttered assent and a small silence whilst Lyse digested this unexpected promotion. She had a sudden disturbing recall of the Labour Party branch meetings of her thirties: tea and minutes for the women and policy making for the men. She was torn between laughing aloud and giving in to genuine disappointment.

"Well, Mr Chairman, thanks for the offer but I don't really see myself as a minute man or woman," she said stiffly, laying aside the book and pen on a littered table at her elbow.

Wilfred shuffled and creaked in his chair. He took off his thick rimmed glasses and polished them on his shirt ends.

"Women always do the minutes." he looked honestly puzzled, "Why else would you be asked?"

Lyse flushed, disappointment giving way to amusement. From the corner of her eye she saw Smiler throw a sly smirk across at Prosser who snorted and buried his nose in his cup. Kilt emptied a quarter bottle of water into a stained mug and mixed in a small helping of whiskey,

"Here," he said. "Save this wee dram for later. No harm in writing us up just this one time, is there?"

Their eyes met briefly. His were conciliatory, dark blue and extraordinarily round and protruding. At least one of them had the grace to look embarrassed and for his sake, Lyse nodded, "OK. This once and thanks Kilt," she continued after a significant pause, "but if I drink whiskey I take it neat like the rest of you."

＊＊

Lyse and Cassie

By the time Lyse had finished her account she realised they were at the ice cream and coffee stage. She had surprised herself. When had she last talked like this with anyone? Not recently. Not since Dian's clever, quick witted conversation had deserted them both. Her eyes filled as she considered the loss of what they had once taken for granted: their hectic to and fro of talk, their word play and catch phrases, all gone now, drowned in the sticky glue of Dian's failing brain.

She looked down and forced the tears to stay behind her lids and then smiled across at Cassie, who sat choking with mirth and waving her long spoon undecidedly between the chocolate and the strawberry.

"Lyse you strident feminist wench and what a liar, liar, pants on fire! You never touch alcohol." Cassie drained her glass. "Good for you, I suppose. So back to the greenhouse is it now? Have you done with them? They sound absolutely primitive."

"Well, I've decided to give them another chance. Perhaps I can civilise them." Lyse suppressed a habitual glance at her watch and jumped right into the unknown of the outside world of after nine o'clock.

"Tell you what, have another drink if you want. I'll have more coffee and then... then," she hesitated only briefly, "I'll give you a lift home, if you like."
"You bet I like," said Cassie, and signalled for another glass, "I've left my bike at the local station. It'll give me time to sober up." She pointed her spoon across the table, "and I like this Lyse, our old Lyse. You've been gone too long girl."

Chapter Three:

Ruby

Ruby filled her special glass vase with water and then began to strip leaves from the flowers Robert and her grandchildren had brought with them. All was quiet again. There would be nothing to keep her company apart from the ticking clock for the rest of the day. Sternly she reminded herself that she was lucky. How much time had they given their own parents when they had been the busy ones? Not nearly enough.

The dinner things lay in wait for her on the drainer but she continued to ignore them. The dark red and burnt orange dahlias were beautiful but almost scentless. She would go and cut some sweet peas in the garden. The dishes could wait. Over five years had passed but still she missed their married Sunday after dinner togetherness: the shared washing up and their bird spotting competition through the kitchen window. The old Collins bird book was now placed handily on the sill and no longer concealed in his bedside drawer. The rotten cheat - her Douglas had never liked to lose.

She stood the vase on the centre table mat and carefully arranged her few birthday cards on either side. She glanced across at the dresser where another was tucked behind a stand-up calendar. Suddenly she was anxious to remove it from its hiding place and to display it in plain sight. This was silly. It was just a birthday card, not a guilty secret.

The envelope was thick and creamy and like the card was of good quality. It was nothing like the flimsy last minute ones from the old box at *The Cabin* Dian had kept for emergencies. She shook out the card and read the stilted formal little message inside.

"To dear Ruby Winters with best wishes William Wilson."

With a small sigh of pleasure she read again the embossed letters on the front cover: "To a Special Friend."

William

William examined the contents of the kitchen cupboard with a sigh: soup, beans and those endless cartons of jelly and custard that Lyse Connor always brought along with her. She must have read somewhere that people with dementia found them digestible but Dian had no idea what to do with a spoon anymore. Everything in the cupboard needed a spoon or a fork. He supposed that if he asked, Lyse would have read up on what to do about that too. He shut the door far harder than he had intended and it sprang back. This time he closed it carefully and levered himself away from the work surface and limped across to the fridge to find only one medium cheese and tomato pizza or the shop bought sandwiches. They had eaten the other pizza for lunch, so sandwiches then. The freezer was empty of ready meals. He pictured the way it had once been stacked with dozens of home prepared dinners, all clearly labelled. He remembered also, how he had resented them and the weekday absence of his wife. They were the good old days though compared to now. He would have to try and find another quiet moment and do an on-line shop. That had proven more complicated than he had thought, what with the constant interruptions from Dian and the overwhelming choice on offer.

Perhaps he should think of getting in more help than Social Services gave them. Were there still such people as housekeepers these days? It would have to be someone who could do more than cook and shop, someone who would know how to handle Dian. He quickly dismissed the idea as impossible and returned to organising their meagre supper.

He shook out the sandwiches, cut them into quarters and sliced off Dian's crusts before switching on the kettle. A small frisson of unease crept into his consciousness as he contemplated a time in the not too distant future when she would forget how to pick up a sandwich. Well at least that was not today.

He pulled open the cupboard again, hoping to find something extra they could have and scanned the shelves without conviction. Finally he noticed the square old fashioned tin with a Christmas holly and ivy pattern stamped on the lid.

"Just a little thank you for all the lifts you've been giving me, "Ruby had said, "for your tea, and for Dian of course."

He lifted the lid and for a mad moment felt as if Christmas had indeed come. Inside was an unexpected kindness in the shape of a half dozen sugar frosted welsh cakes and a couple of plump current scones.

How thoughtful. Dear Ruby, such a special friend. What would he do without her?

Chapter Four:

Lyse and Elora

Lyse was one of the last in the allotment. Most people had slowly packed up and left for their dinner whilst she had continued to weed her raised beds, revelling in the gradual emptying of human life leaving her with just bird song and the lengthening mid summer evening.

As she twisted old newspapers into faggots and added thin strips of kindling and twigs for the bonfire bin Lyse's glance occasionally strayed to a carrier bag she had brought with her.

Keep or burn Dian's old love letters? Rereading them after so long had consoled and hurt. They had brought to life the woman Dian had been, the one she rarely glimpsed these days.

On her latest visit, Dian's cloudy eyes had cleared for a moment. Oblivious to the presence of her husband she had taken Lyse by the hand and proclaimed, "*Oh, lover comes!*" Erica had moved swiftly, noisily greeting Dian and asking William to help her into the kitchen with the bag of lunch things she had prepared, tactfully taking him away from that incendiary sentence which had dropped, like a grenade, the pin pulled, between them in the hallway.

Dian had fondly imagined their love affair had been a "delicious secret" although Lyse was convinced that Erica and probably William had also known. There was a certain kind of look in those sad brown eyes of his, a look of injured distaste whenever they fleetingly met hers that confirmed her suspicions. Would it be kinder to him if she burnt all those mementoes? Did she owe him that much at least? Postponing that decision she hurried towards the shed to hunt out her box of extra long Swan matches, as if it was possible to walk away from that shared past and all the heartache it had unpleasantly brought into their present.

Half way along the path she slowed her pace and then stopped. There was a part view of a slender someone in a pair of knee length dungarees and green wellingtons. A long dark ponytail hanging between bare tanned shoulders was just visible but the face was hidden by the open door. This was definitely not one of the usual inhabitants. Most bore an uncanny clone-like similarity to the committee, as did their plots of rigid rows of vegetables with hardly a fruit bush and never a flower in sight.

Before she could call out the face withdrew from inside the shed. It was heart shaped and framed by an over large pair of glasses. As the visitor noticed Lyse who had resumed her progress along the rough grassy track she called up to her with a wide smile full of perfect white teeth.

"Are you Lyse?" she said and held out a grubby hand when Lyse arrived, "I'm Elora, from Plot 28."

Lyse shook hands, "How can I help you?" she said, instantly recognising an echo of the usual perfunctory greeting she had often given to surprise callers at her office door. She tried again, "How nice, a guest. Come on in and have a cup of tea. I hope you don't mind it from a flask."

"I don't mind if I do," the younger woman smiled wide and hopped up the three steps and once inside promptly unfolded a canvas chair. She threw herself into it and stretched out her long booted legs as if exhausted.

Lyse gave a quick grin in return. What an infectious smile. How old? Perhaps she could be mid-thirties, or a little older, Sal's age? "Have you taken over one of the vacant plots by the gate?" she asked and passed a plastic cup with a rueful grimace, "sorry, it's a bit stewed."

"Wet and warm," returned Elora and raised her tea in salute, "or so my Dad always used to say." She gave a small suggestive giggle, "I was never sure if he was talking about tea or girl friends, the wicked old dog!"

After taking a moment to process the innuendo, Lyse spluttered into her cup and gave a rusty, unaccustomed hoot of laughter.

"Sorry," said Elora, "that was a bit cheeky and I so wanted to give you the right impression. I think I may need your help."

"Oh?" Lyse was intrigued. Had someone suggested that she was a go to person for gardening advice? It was hardly likely.

"You are on the committee, right?" Elora pulled a much creased and mud stained note from the wide chest pocket in her dungarees and handed it to Lyse.

Lyse eyed the paper warily then reluctantly opened it. "Well, I went to one meeting but I'm not sure that..." she broke off as she read the official heading in bold capitals: NON CULTIVATION ORDER. She had heard them talk about sending these out, had faithfully recorded the decision in the minutes, but had heard no mention of this reason hand printed in red ink on a dotted line underneath: TOO MANY FLOWERS.

She looked up, puzzled, "You're joking, aren't you?"

Elora gave her head a vigorous shake, her pony tail sweeping back and forth like a young colt's. Lyse studied the letter and then Elora. Belying her casual demeanour, tears glinted behind the younger woman's spectacles.

Her own plot had flowers, fruit and vegetables. She had grass paths, not paving slabs. There were no regimented rows measured for the correct distance, or labels, nor a strict rotation plan. No one had ever said anything to her, she never won plot of the year of course, but only the same old few ever did. Two of whom had signed this letter: Wilfred James and Don Wantz.

"Well, it's not 1945, and we're not digging for Britain." She poured more tea" adding diplomatically," but I think it's usual to grow a mixture of flowers, fruit and veg."

"Oh, I grow everything, everything I can think of." Elora took off her glasses and quickly wiped her eyes with the back of her hand, "but I just don't grow like they do – see." Taking out another folded paper she handed over an exquisite line drawing, washed with faint water colour.

"Why it's wonderful Elora. You could frame this."

Obviously pleased Elora shrugged, ""I want to grow things but to make something... something wild and beautiful at the same time." Her face fell, "I thought I had, but perhaps not."

In the silence that followed Lyse pretended not to notice the tears still occasionally escaping from behind the glass and stood up.

"I bet *it is* wild and beautiful," she said, "why don't we take a walk down there now and you can show me round.

***

It was still early in the growing year but it was immediately obvious to Lyse that Elora's desire to "create something wild and wonderful" was well under way. There was nothing of the random in the marigolds amongst the tomatoes and basil, the cabbages and rosemary, the bean and pea plugs cheerfully sitting next to the future promise of lupins and sweet peas.

Lyse lingered, fascinated and envious, admiring every raised bed; the battered buckets full of seedlings and former orange boxes full of fledgling nasturtiums just about to cascade their bright yellow and orange face like flowers over the edges. It reminded her of an old postcard Dian had sent her from New England once: an eighteenth century painting depicting Native Americans intercropping planting around their homes. All that was missing in Elora's garden were the teepees.

As she looked up to smile her approval she realised that, until that moment she had missed the tall oblong of a makeshift shed cleverly decorated to resemble Dr Who's telephone box.

Lyse made a cautious approach and carefully pulled on the door knob afraid the whole thing might fall down but it was surprisingly sturdy. An old fashioned deckchair and an upturned packing case covered by a white lace table cloth made up the furnishings. There was also an open bird cage with a cat saucer full of sunflower seeds hanging from the ceiling by a huge black hook.

Had she walked into some kind of time warp? As if reading her mind Elora said, "My Dad was a scene painter and this was one of the last things he made me. For years it lived in our garage, but I think it looks good up here, as if it's in its rightful place, don't you?"

Lye stepped inside and examined the sketches and magazine pictures Blu tacked onto a children's display board. At the back of her mind she was also processing just how much everything about Elora and her amazing space would unsettle and irritate those blinkered old dinosaurs and all their like-minded mates. A sudden intuition prompted her to ask:

"Who has the bigger piece of this land bordering yours?"

"Oh, him," Elora pulled a face, "That's Barry. He says weeds shouldn't be allowed."

"Well, we all think that but they just keep on growing." Lyse responded with practised statesmanship and quickly changed the subject. "Don't they call him Barry Island?"

"Yes, but he isn't nice, like the real Barry Island. He's always telling me I'm not a proper gardener and I should give up and let him put my ground to good use for his potato crop."

Lyse looked through the plastic covered window and studied the adjoining plot. Barry was only just visible as he knelt amongst his early lettuces, weeding no doubt. There was a huge pile of wood and other rubbish stacked quite close to the rope that separated their land.

Elora, following her gaze, shrugged, "He's always lighting those fires. He never uses a bin and I swear he waits until the wind is blowing in my direction."

Was the truth of the matter just a good old fashioned piece of land grabbing then? As if to confirm her suspicions Barry's head and shoulders lifted to greet his visitors: Wilfred James and Smiler. The three stood together in a huddle, sharing cigarettes and throwing occasional glances in their direction.

"Can I keep this letter and drawing for a day or two?" Lyse asked, conviction hardening her already half formed resolve to bite the bullet and take them on, "I expect we'll find it's all a storm in a tea cup.

***

On her arrival home one of the first things Lyse did was to call Cassie. After twenty minutes she replaced the handset, smiling broadly. Cassie had responded in exactly the way she had imagined on her walk home. Sometimes she reminded her strongly of her Dian of old.

"Bamboozle them with horticultural science old girl. Wave their own constitution at them and..." Cassie had admonished, "Stick to your guns!"

What she had not expected though was the pressing invitation to supper for the following evening, or her own ready acceptance. What had Cassie meant by "That's a date then?" Could they really step back a decade and try again? Was she any less scared, her heart less battered? She moved a little closer to the long dress mirror that had once graced Dian's town house and scrutinised the dishevelled woman that looked back. When had she last bothered to take a good look at herself? No wonder Mum was always suggesting they should share a Spa Day. Tomorrow was Friday. Was there still time to put right the careless cut of her hair, the unkempt eyebrows, the ragged and soil rimmed nails, perhaps have a facial?

The unexpectedness of the day had left her with a pleasant feeling of bemused self- awareness. For once she had allowed herself to enjoy the company of an attractive and intriguing younger woman and had then accepted a dinner invitation from an older but equally captivating one.

As she fussed her kitten George and searched the fridge for something quick and easy for them both her memory was busy trying to locate vague fragments of a poem about being surprised by joy. Wordsworth, she guessed. Retirement was already making her rusty. It took a while but eventually she located the opening line: "Surprised by joy – impatient as the Wind." Elora- a welcome breath of fresh air, but...

But the poem's theme had quickly turned away from joy to a grief briefly blown aside by the breeze and sparkle of a beautiful day. At first Lyse was pleased and reassured by her powers of recall but almost in the next breath her spirits dropped to their habitual low. All her earlier excited plans stalled, hitting that eternal mountain of guilt and anxiety that seemed to lay across her shoulders like the load carried by Atlas.

She knew, deep down, that there was nothing to feel guilty about. Friendship between her and Dian had existed far longer even than their love affair. Meeting Cassie the first time round had been years after those days. Cassie was undeniably attractive but her sexuality seemed so ambiguous and taking another chance like that would be madness. Anyway, she was too old and luckily her heart no longer lived on her sleeve.

Lyse shook off her pointless introspections and called her mother who, when told the tale had counselled that a bit of war paint never went amiss when dealing with ruthless poachers of land and suggested they visit her favourite beauty parlour "ASAP."

By the time she was ready for bed she locked and bolted the doors and pulled the curtains together with a decisive swish assuring herself that the make-over was just "ammunition" and nothing to do with young women or so-called dates with the mercurial Cassie.

Chapter Five:

Erica

As Erica buckled up and sat back in the passenger seat she calculated that they must have made this monthly visit for over three years. Her heart sank at the thought that on this trip, like every other, they would find less of the Dian they remembered. It was just one endless long goodbye. She looked across at her companion and toyed with the desire to share her thoughts but quickly dismissed the idea. It was hard for her but obviously far harder for Lyse.

Of course that shared history between those two did not help the difficulties with William. His monosyllabic often defensive responses to even the mildest of queries from Lyse were frustrating. On the other hand Lyse was only too ready to pick on any small perceived example of neglect and would often rant all the way back to the car park. Erica was weary after one of her inexplicable sleepless nights and fervently hoped that he would go out or at least upstairs and free them from an afternoon of oppressive halting conversation that had them all, including Dian, covertly eyeing the clock willing it to reach four.

Unaware of her friend's melancholy mood Lyse turned and held out her fist to be bumped as was their routine and intoned grimly: "Onwards and upwards!" Erica eyed Lyse with a curious sharp look. There was something different about her today but she could not quite pin it down.

"Do you like the new look?" said Lyse, "Mum persuaded me to have a silver rinse. You know what she's like, still such a fashion diva."

Erica, usually a firm believer in *au naturel* had to admit that the colour worked and somehow lightened Lyse's overall appearance. She noted the smart jeans and the neatly pressed blue shirt, the clean well manicured nails as Lyse pressed the ignition. The scuffed trainers had been replaced by a pair of soft leather ankle boots that Erica remembered well from her former smart work day wear.

Lyse grinned, reading her mind, "It's called ammunition."

Erica raised an enquiring eyebrow, "ammunition?"

"It's a long story."

Erica settled back relieved by Lyse's unanticipated cheery air. She fought the urge to close her eyes and ruminated vaguely on air fresheners. There was always a faint whiff of allotment odour in Lyse's cars. Would a Christmas gift of selected deodorizers offend? Probably.

"Well we've got fourteen miles," she said, "Start from the beginning."

Lyse told her tale with a relish she rarely showed these days. She described the quixotic Elora and the awful letter stating that she grew TOO MANY FLOWERS; the capitals somehow depicting their innocent beauty as a cardinal sin! She faltered for a moment and the pleasure in telling her story flagged. The original postcard from Dian was in her bag but there would probably be little point in getting it out. Dian was beginning to show scant interest in anything and spent most of the time pacing to the window and back, making incomprehensible comments about the weather or people passing by.

With an effort she pushed away that painful thought, describing instead, Elora's clever sketch and their successful open Sunday at Plot 28. She confessed to having done a gleeful little jig after the "motley crew" as Elora called them, had retreated under the barrage of Cassie's practical ammunition. Her war paint being a pointless exercise, she confessed. She mentioned the scowls of Barry Island and his illegal lighting of another fire in an effort to smoke out their visitors but censored his muttered comments about "flaky feminist lesboes." Lyse teetered on the edge of remarking that befriending Elora had transformed her afternoon gardening sessions and waxed over- lyrical about companion planting instead.

As she drew to the curb and switched off she saw Dian who, as always, was kneeling on the sofa and staring through the wide bay window as if searching for something or someone. She waved. Dian's greeting in return was hesitant and brief. She turned and was gone. Lyse sighed and glanced across at Erica whose eyes were closed hands folded loosely in her lap. She leaned closer and studied the relaxed features and a little panicky, looked for the reassuring rise and fall of a beating heart, jerking back with an exclamation as Erica snapped open an eye.

"Just resting my eyes," said Erica with a thin amused smile, "that all sounds like a very satisfying outcome." She stepped into the road and then ducked her head back inside and considered her friend shrewdly.

"I'm sure your war paint won't go unnoticed by either of those interesting women." She said, giving Lyse a kindly speculative look. "Good for you. It's time you had some fun."

Lyse flushed and hurried to the boot where she buried her head feeling ridiculously like a schoolgirl caught out by a headmistress. Was she really that transparent to everyone except herself? Erica's comments echoed Cassie's who had asked during their meal "Can't you let yourself have a little fun darling Lyse?" Later, as they made their goodbyes Cassie had rested her hands on her shoulders and asked, quite seriously for her, "If we kiss will it hurt you?"

She cringed at the toe curling reminder of the way she had jumped backwards as if struck by a venomous snake. Relived the silly joke she had mumbled about teenagers, doorsteps and having forgotten "how to" before having leapt through the gate and into her car; heard again the screech and squeal of her brakes as she fled the scene.

Finally she closed the boot and joined Erica who had already pressed the bell. Questions she knew she had been ducking for weeks followed close on her heels: was her heart's best treasure still the sad shadow behind the glass? Could she remain tied to a woman who no longer even remembered her name? Did she, had she ever, done fun when it came to romance? Was that what was missing in her life?

The fortress door, sharply withdrew its bolt and the lock beneath it clicked to open. Lyse caught a glimpse of Dian's curious and diffident expression peeping from behind William's stooping and bulky frame. Those vague questions were instantly transformed into an unwelcome, piercing insight. It was possible, as Cassie had delicately hinted that Dian had become someone to hide behind: an excuse begun even long before the dreaded Alzheimer's had made itself apparent.

***

Dian

Dian was once again at her station by the window, her visitors forgotten. She contemplated the empty street, the rows of parked cars, the tall houses opposite and her neglected garden. Her senses dimly registered a difference in the day. The *special one* crossed to the sofa and knelt next to her*. It was a nice ... something...hug?*

Erica half stood, thinking to join them, but instead slid quietly back into the deep tapestry folds of the armchair all at once aware that to watch them would be to pry. Quickly she picked up the newspaper from the coffee table and unobtrusively busied herself with the headlines.

"The weather has gone off," Lyse said, acutely conscious of how dear was the warm touch under her hand and how much missed was the familiar favourite perfume and the once soapy scent of Dian's hair. "See how the wind has got up." Quite naturally Dian moved into the embrace, pressing her cheek against Lyse's own, the foggy light blue of her eyes suddenly clearing. She waved a hand at the view outside and shrugged.

Sticks are bend and back...a swirl and swoosh are now... she pointed at a dustbin lid as it clattered down the street...**all bowled out and over."**

The ugly privet Lyse had always disliked was rocking and bending as the full force of the unexpected squall met it head on. Assorted litter was chasing behind the bin cover and as spits of slanting rain rushed by Dian continued with her uncannily accurate forecast... **wet sprinkles are down... up high black curtains pulled across...blue and yellow gone...**

***

Erica and Lyse

Erica squinted past the streaming rain and the frantic scraping back and forth of her over worked wipers. Somehow she managed to navigate their way safely off the traffic ridden single lane of the town and onto the motorway. This was ridiculously near-tropical rainfall of epic proportions even for Britain. Steve would undoubtedly lay the cause at global warming. It reminded her of the kind of flash flooding she had only ever witnessed when they were living in the States. By some miracle she had never found herself driving through one before, had always been a safe and comfortable bystander usually safely behind a floor to ceiling window with a panoramic vista to thrill and admire. Now she regretted having left at their usual time. Why had she airily insisted that it was her turn to drive back and that the poor driving conditions would present her with no problems? Had she just been so desperate to get away from William...from Dian?

The entire journey, even in the comparative safety of the inside lane of the M4, stretched her tired mind to the limit. The deafening crescendo of rain and wipers prevented any meaningful conversation, her passenger almost forgotten until the car park was reached and a vacant slot located. Thankfully she pulled up the handbrake and switched off.

The rain still drummed and bounced mercilessly off the roof but without the added racket of the wipers the silence between them was suddenly palpable. Erica's face was unusually pale and strained. Belatedly and guilty, Lyse glance across and immediately registered the difficulties of the drive for Erica. She should never have let Erica drive her car in all that weather. But how on earth could she have stopped her once her mind was made up?

"Fancy running in for a coffee?" she suggested, sorry she had not offered one scrap of support or encouragement throughout the journey, ashamed of having been completely wrapped up inside her own muddled thoughts, "You deserve one. That was a courageous feat!"

Erica sighed. The drive had been a beast but it was the visit that had left her feeling more than usually helpless and despondent. She tugged at her skirt and picked at a nonexistent thread, surprising herself with a sudden rush of tears that she was unable to stop falling and splashing, like a parody of the rain, onto her hands.

Lyse stared at her friend, at first puzzled and then contrite. For a moment she felt oddly, selfishly, cast adrift, before hurriedly handing over a clean cotton handkerchief. She sat quietly allowing her friend to cry, awkwardly patting her arm from time to time listening to Erica's broken explanations: her horror at the pace of the disease, the way there was less of Dian with every visit, her desperate need to talk to her best friend now that her own life had become so inexplicably complicated.

As they hurried towards the cafe, huddled together under Erica's skimpy umbrella, Lyse had to acknowledge that their always unlikely friendship had taken a sudden seismic shift. From now on she would remember that these visits to Dian were just as painful for Erica. Her loss was not the only one that counted. How on earth could she take Dian's place as close friend and confidante? It was going to take far more than a cup of coffee in a cinema's cafe.

Chapter Six:

Ruby
The Tea Dance

Ruby had taken far longer than usual in front of the mirror, had used more than a quick scrape of face powder and a mere hint of lipstick. She had also spent far more than intended on the new dress and then extra on a visit to the hairdresser. The full length mirror, long ignored, reflected back at her a woman she hardly recognised. She gave it a shy glance, and then another, and then a longer harder look. Was it possible that she liked what she saw? Or was it just the lovely lavender-grey silky feel of the dress and the colour rinse in her hair? The last time she had worn anything this nice was on their fortieth wedding anniversary. The silver dancing shoes and the matching clutch bag had been presents from Douglas. He had loved to dance. He would have thought a Harvest Festival Tea Dance a great idea. Yes, she reassured herself, he would have approved of this expense. He had always liked her "nicely turned out" as he had called it, sounding just like his father. She sighed. She would have to look for a different partner this afternoon. Were William's dancing days over? Had they ever begun? Would he ask her? Would she dare ask him, if not?

The unexpected double chime of the doorbell caused her to take a guilty step away from the mirror as if her visitor would somehow guess she had been indulging in a silly vain daydream. It was too early for her lift. Ruby hurried to the window and looked down at the open gate. It was Robert, on a work day? She hesitated and then slipped on her shoes and picked up her bag.

"Robert! What are you doing here? Is anything wrong?" Ruby had only partly opened the door and after a moment reluctantly moved aside to let him in, "I'm just on my way out."

"I had a delivery in the area," he said, his smile fading at this lukewarm greeting and the unexpected loss of a quick sandwich before his long drive back, "I thought I'd just pop in. I thought you'd be pleased."

"Of course I'm pleased love," Ruby gave him a belated peck on the cheek, resisting a quick check of her watch. "Come on in and I'll put the kettle on. I might have time to make you a ham sandwich and I think there's some cake left in the tin."

Robert threw himself into a kitchen chair suddenly recognising the action and the whine in his tone as the one belonging to his old teenage self who had hated not to be the centre of his mother's attention.

"You look very nice Mum," he said, making an effort, "Are you going anywhere special?"

"It's the..." Ruby broke off as she heard the sharp blast of the car horn. Immediately she set down the bread knife pushing it across to her son, oddly determined to prevent William from coming to the door.

"I must dash. You can look after yourself can't you dear?" She said and practically fled down the hall offering a final flustered explanation over her shoulder, "The tea dance will be without its tea if I don't get that old urn going as soon as possible."

Through the living room window Robert watched thoughtfully as an elderly man leaned across and opened the passenger door. He noted the familiar way they greeted each other. As he moved back into the kitchen to finish his own ham sandwich his thick-set eyebrows creased and met in the middle not unlike his father's. Her attention was very definitely elsewhere today.

It had been a long time since he had seen her so smart. Was that a new dress, a different hairdo? Just to serve tea at the old folks Tea Dance? The figure had been somewhat obscured by the nets but he was sure it was William Wilson who used to run the after school club years ago. He had that wife with the unusual name who could beat anyone off the dart board. Was he a widower now: Mr Wilson and his Mum? His frown deepened and then cleared: no, never in a million years.

William

William hardly ever noticed his surroundings but even he felt a flush of pride at the way their moderately sized, moderately well kept community hall looked today. The cheerful bunting, last used for the Queen's Jubilee, brightened and partially hid the scuffed paintwork of the walls and the globe paper lanterns concealed the bare light bulbs, giving the old floor boards at least the illusion of a dance floor. Already the tables and chairs were being pushed further against the walls to allow more room. For once the refreshments appeared to be the second favourite, even though the cakes were piled temptingly high and the faint whiff of warm sausage rolls strongly echoed the pavement lure of a Greggs at lunch time.

William gratefully moved towards the counter. He had missed lunch and probably breakfast too. The new carers seemed to come later every morning and then the battle of trying to get Dian out of bed and agreeing to a semblance of a wash would begin. He had only just managed to get away in time to pick Ruby up. Credit for today had to go to Ruby and a few others on the committee who had not only worked hard on the decorating and food but had come up with the idea of using a real band this year instead of the usual poorly taped reproductions. Now this was what you could call a Tea Dance.

The Mad Hatters, a sexagenarian quartet in top hats, spats and tails, had certainly brought in the crowds as their flyer had promised. Couples were taking to the dance floor with an enthusiasm seldom witnessed for years. Hopefully the old flooring which was already bouncing and bending under the strain would hold out until seven!

As his good foot tapped along to a catchy old fashioned repertoire his parents would have recognised from the in between war years he vaguely wondered when he had last danced to live music or even to the usual substandard offerings of their annual Summer Dance afternoon. He and Dian had often gone to theatres and onto dances in the West End in their early days. He had never been a confident dancer although he had a hazy remembrance of enjoying showing off his young and attractive wife. She had soon tired of him treading on her feet though and had always waltzed or jived away with one or another willing partner cheerfully blowing him a parting kiss.

Back in his habitual corner he wolfed down his plate of sandwiches and glanced across to where Ruby was still behind the counter serving teas, an apron covering that nice outfit he had never seen before. She was certainly dressed for the occasion and so was everyone else it seemed. William was suddenly conscious that he had on his crumpled every day suit and had not even bothered to change his shirt or shine his shoes and for once it mattered. Perhaps he could slip home and change before the Hatters had their midway break. Inexplicably he began to feel a ridiculous impulse to dance, to join in the fun and forget about the grey, fraught, rest of his life for a while.

With a dogged determination he held onto his empty plate and threaded his way through the dancers and back to the counter, his mind frantically rehearsing how to phrase a casual offer to sign Ruby's dance card.

"Hello William," said Ruby taking his plate, giving him that kind welcoming hazel eyed smile he found so comforting, "I've managed to save you a piece of your favourite Victoria sponge."
"Ruby!" William blurted, far louder than he had intended, his muted polite request forgotten. "You look far too nice in that lovely dress to waste all your time serving tea and cakes. I've just got to run home and change into some decent clothes before I can ask to sign your dance card."

Embarrassed and aware that the curious eyes of one or two helpers had turned their way he amended, "Ah, that is if you would care to - or with someone else perhaps."

Ruby carefully put down the cake tin, conscious of the interest William's impromptu speech had caused, and also of a small absurd girlish flutter of pleasure inside. She rummaged for a moment in her pocket before pulling out her folded and empty dance card.

"Don't bother to change William," she said, briskly untying her apron strings, ignoring the covert looks from Cilla and Dawn, tea towels suspended, just inside the kitchen "take off your jacket and maybe the tie and give me a minute. Lucky I saved you a couple. There are a few quicksteps coming up next. Do you think you can manage them?"

"Oh yes, I think so." They traded a quick conspiratorial look before throwing caution to the wind as William added, "I can also do a mean fox trot when pushed."

Chapter Seven:

Lyse

Lyse looked down the long length of their table and then at the one adjacent with another dozen or so former staff and colleagues. In just two years? How was it possible? Not long ago most of these people had seemed more familiar and closer to her than members of her own family.

She began to name count the heads and their connected arms reaching out for food whilst busy catching up or exuberantly greeting late comers. From behind the tall candle sticks and mounds of saffron rice and other tasty dishes she spotted Eve of course: they had only ever tolerated each other– now they exchanged a polite obligatory nod. There was Billy. He never usually came along to this kind of thing but there he sat among the women still wearing a grubby baseball cap with a knot of scruffy greying hair pulled through the back. They gave each other the friendly thumbs up. She turned her attention to the further end where the reason for this little party was opening an ungainly package tied with a red ribbon and a balloon upon which some wag had written in felt tip: "You're off then … at last!" Eileen, their trusty Head of payroll and computer whizz was the last to leave before their old much loved but crumbling building was closed forever.

Across the way; behind more elaborate candlesticks and shiny decorative tableware was Marie who had somehow wangled a night off from the three children. Erica was seated nearby, her white head cocked, dutifully trying to follow her neighbour's ceaseless conversation. Only Debs would try and compete with the wailing lament and tinny piped sitar music plus dozens of mainly high feminine voices plainly having a really good time.

Jenny, was that another new hairdo, nudged Lyse and said, "I think Eileen is going to give a speech." Eileen was holding a dinner fork aloft and a glass in her other hand. The incessant chatter slowly hummed to a standstill and all expectant eyes turned to where she stood, larger than life in personality and size, decked out in an extraordinary floral two piece.

"Well," whispered Lyse, "She's worn some outfits in her time but this one beats the lot!"

Jenny put her finger to her lips and Rose, complacent in her unchallenged role as fashion diva suppressed a grin and shook her head, "Now old new boss quit with that talk!"

An over loud text alert suddenly punctuated the silence. Lyse frantically began searching her pockets, throwing an apologetic look down the table, hoping to shut it off before it began again. Barely a minute later: there was another ping. This time it was Erica playing out the same search pantomime, surreptitiously upending her handbag between her feet.

"I see management have found new ways to silence me!" Eileen quipped, drawing wild applause, "however, unaccustomed as I am ..." Lyse's mobile began a chorus of William Tell. She declined but within a second another text alert clamoured for her attention.

Ann and Anna
(The Texts)

Please call. We are upset and worried about Dian. The A's

We are at a lunch party. Can we call later? L & E

Please call now. Cant wait.

I'll call in ten. L

NOW

Lyse hastily read the texts and then resolutely powered off. Erica scanned and replied to a similar set of messages before pressing the red button folding the phone back into her bag.

On the pretext of a half standing stretch she managed to send Lyse their old work place palms down wait awhile signal. Obviously it was not quite life or death and this was Eileen's afternoon. Whatever it was it had to wait until the dessert stage at least.

***

Dian and William
(Earlier that day)

William hurries Dian from the car and back to the ramp. He places her hand on the iron bar and leaves her to climb alone as he fumbles up himself, dragging his lame leg impatiently. He punches the bell two, three times as Dian carefully negotiates the unfamiliar walkway, stretching her arms awkwardly between the newly installed railings.

Man angry...how help it? This wide...too long...need to...need too...how wait it?

Dian stands irresolute, one step outside the open door lifting a foot and then the other, clutching the front of her skirt watching as William stomps back to the car. She turns to...

Who these...where is...who these...these are... these are A's yes A's...I know these...

She turns to the figures in the doorway. Her heart rate slows, her sudden fear subsides, the tall door takes shape again and these faces are smiling. Outstretched hands gentle her inside with voices soft and calm. She tries for an explanation, searches for hidden words to explain her need. Her pressing need to...

My water will falls...pee on leg...on shoe...on inside shoe...man angry...how help it?

As Dian's need overwhelms her fragile control she stares down at her feet as water runs from beneath her skirt, as droplets splinter across her shoes and pool onto the floor. Dian cries, the A's cry too.

***

Erica

Erica sat for a while in her driveway, absently picking at her skirt with one hand and pressing a finger between her eyebrows with the other. Somehow that happy gathering of former colleagues had disintegrated into the beginnings of a particularly vicious headache. She sighed and snapped open the seat belt thinking it was probably a good thing that Stephen would still be out for at least another hour. He was bound to ask whether she had read the brochures he had left on the kitchen table. Perhaps she should try for a nap? Her stress levels would never allow that. Perhaps she should try a large glass of something alcoholic for a change then?

Once in doors she paused only to kick off her shoes and made for the dining room where they kept what they laughingly called their cocktail bar. In reality it was her mother's old glass cabinet containing oddments of Waterford crystal and whatever was left over from Christmas, christenings and birthdays. Erica picked up the remains of a bottle of red and gave it a dubious sniff before putting it down, settling instead for a tumbler and a generous helping of good scotch. She toyed with the idea of going into the kitchen to look for a mixer or at least some ice but the swift reminder of why she was drinking in the middle of the afternoon hit her full force causing her to empty the glass in two quick gulps.

She gasped in protest. The smoky peaty taste bit at her tongue before miraculously turning silky smooth, instantly dialling down her jangled nerves and calming her headache.

Pouring herself another she crossed to the far end of the room and sank down into an armchair with a good view of her favourite silver birch. For a long moment she schooled herself to focus solely on the delicate papery quality of its ancient bark, the triangular green canopy and the light blue early autumn sky behind. Had she managed to persuade Lyse not to hurtle down the motorway? Was she, at this very moment, tearing her way there like an avenging angel from hell? No, Lyse had given her word, had eventually seen the sense of not creating a conflict that could cause them to lose all contact with Dian. Had the A's - was it Ann and Annie, or Anna – carried out their threat to resign? Hopefully she had, at least, talked them out of calling the police.

It was definitely not quite the crime they thought it was but still, was there any excuse for what he had done? Was it really the unkind and callous action it appeared to be? Dian had never suggested that he was worse than rather dense and uncommunicative. She had always implied that their marriage was merely one of long habit and convenience. Was he a plausible villain or merely a man out of his depth, needing help, no matter what the others may think?

She slowly sipped at her drink and contemplated her happy forty odd years with Stephen. What kind of marriage would someone have to have to withstand the ravages of a disease like Alzheimer's? After all, even their solid alliance seemed to be faltering lately and for far less reason. What advice would Dian offer if only it was possible? Something witty and slyly profound in their cod- French no doubt.

"Humour l'homme mon cher sinon comment garder la paix," was that right?

Her drink finished she crossed to the window at the creak of the gate on its rusty hinges. She waved to her husband. Yes her darling husband, in his familiar old jacket and those awful unfamiliar blue jeans and ridiculous brand name trainers. Her heart lifted as he quickened his pace and waved a newspaper in return. Keeping the peace she could do, but calling him Steve, never. That was just too beyond the pale.

"I've been looking at those brochures," she lied brightly, opening the door before his key had half turned in the lock, "I think you might have a point. Come and have a cup of tea and talk me through them.

***

Lyse

Lyse did not tear down the motorway regardless of speed limits and consequences. Instead she borrowed Nicky's Kelpie pup Roo and took him on a long hike through the bypass. After two hours her mind was still almost incoherent with helpless rage. Eventually she turned for home following the progress of a once abundant stream, throwing sticks for the young dog with a force and a vehemence that had him galloping thrilled and yelping through the murky water. Lyse followed navigating carefully across its slimy stony bottom finding a perverse satisfaction as rushing ankle deep icy cold water filled her socks and boots.

Clock watching for the rest of the evening she counted down the hours of her ferocity, until she grew worried about her sanity, or her blood pressure. She cooked food she was unable to eat and half completed tasks that held no interest until she finally gave up and sat with George on her knee watching the fading red of sunset turn orange and then a pale yellow before it disappeared behind the distant tree line of her garden.

As her fury cooled and her mind's clamour slowly sifted her thoughts into a slow burn of clarity she realised that her rage was not directed solely at William. They were all angry with him, of course they were. Of all things, this afternoon would have wounded Dian in a way that would leave her crushed and diminished still further. It would be an unmending scar that would defy the memory loss of her disease. How *could she* have entrusted her vulnerable self into the care of a man whose deficiencies she must have known only too well? How *dare she* have dismissed any attempts to discuss her decision whilst rational discussion had still been possible!

The white heat of her reawakening anger quickly turned from Dian and inward, scalding its way into her heart. It was *she* who had let Dian go without a fight. It was *she* who must have witnessed a hundred and one acts of accidental neglect almost without protest over the past four years. There was no white horse because *she* had not had the courage to keep her promise. She had become as apathetic and resigned to their fate as Dian seemed to be.

Lyse dropped the protesting George from her knees and ran through the open French doors, stumbled out into the half dark of her garden blindly kicking up the gravel on her dim solar lit pathway. She ran its full length only stopping when the thicket hedge bordering onto the farm prevented her from going further. Oblivious of any thoughts of how far her voice might carry into the quiet night, unmindful of the anxious stamping and shuffling from the shadowy steaming cattle beyond, Lyse, a hard knot twisting beneath her breastbone, hot tears streaking down her face began to yell an incoherent mixture of invective and apologies.

Lyse Remembers

The end tap in the Ladies had been left full on again. Water swirled and gushed down the sink hole, its echoing progress through ancient leaden pipes evidenced by a hollow, decidedly unhealthy sucking noise. Lyse hated the thought of all that water wasted. Would Billy ever replace those difficult twisty taps with the new timed push button ones she had seen delivered to Reception weeks ago? Not if the unattractive shade of yellow remaining on the walls was anything to go by. Large containers of paint had also been part of the delivery and were still stacked in the foyer, just waiting to be stolen by some enterprising student long before Billy ever got round to them.

Lyse crossed to the sink and began to wrestle with the rusting Edwardian tap head but paused, straining to identify the location of the rather melodic whistling now clearly audible as the running tap faded into a half hearted dribble. It must be the same phantom whistler as the one from yesterday and the day before. Lyse grinned, deciding a hasty retreat was in order and tactfully turned the tap back to full pressure. It would be a shame to intrude on what seemed to be an intense personal moment in a very public convenience.

As she moved away from the basins towards the exit the whistling continued but the cubicle door swung open before she could leave.

"Oh, it's you!" said Lyse, her comment spontaneous, her embarrassment acute.

Dian Wilson raised an ironic eyebrow, "Oh, it's you!" she countered, briskly soaping her hands under the tap, only the faintest flush on high cheekbones betraying any discomfort she may have felt with this encounter.

Lyse smiled weakly, wondering why she always seemed to put her foot in it with Dian Wilson. What was it about this classy and cultured older woman who also just happened to be her boss? Why was she always left feeling like a tongue-tied teenager?

"I mean, well I mean to say that whistling is something I've never mastered," she attempted adding unwisely, "It's almost as good as my Grandad's was."

"Your Grandad's!" Dian's light eyes sparked with mischief, "Yes, it's one of those traditional art forms that will probably die out along with us older folk!" she said. The dry sarcasm of her quick witted reply was accompanied by a full on and unexpectedly charming smile that left Lyse slack jawed and ridiculously, hopelessly dazzled.

There was a small awkward silence as the pipes gurgled unpleasantly and as Lyse digested this unexpected epiphany. Dian, only aware that perhaps she had inadvertently offended a little known member of her staff, took refuge behind a joking mock whisper:

"Tout le monde avait leur sensibilite manqué," Lyse struggled with the translation, surely this French was not quite... Dian continued with a wicked grin, "on ne veut pas etre entendu peter en public!"

* * *

The following morning as Lyse dry eyed and shriven, set about completing household chores left undone she reflected again on that early chance meeting which had inexplicably led to such an enduring loving history between them. How long had it taken her younger much smitten self to recognise that behind the witty repertoire of an accomplished court jester was an often shy and vulnerable woman who was prone to the same embarrassments and sensitivities as any other mortal?

As Lyse mindlessly washed dishes and sorted the washing she grew ever more resolute, sifting through the potential pros and cons of her intention. It was not going to please William. Did she care about that? No. Should she ring Erica? No. Erica would advise caution. What good had caution done Dian? No point feeling guilty about keeping Erica out of the loop.

As Lyse hunted out the telephone number she had once scribbled in her address book she pictured the way Dian, just before any controversial intervention, had always employed theatre by picking up a vast imaginary white hat, flicking off its invisible dust, and whistling for her fictional high dudgeon. Lyse's lips set themselves into a determined straight line. Dian deserved better. It was too late for the white horse, but maybe there was still time for the white hat.

Lyse carefully scrutinised the email addressed to William for the fifth time assessing it for diplomacy and a passable imitation of sincere supportive concern. She eventually pressed *Send*. Without that email to cover her back she could hardly justify what she was about to do. To her surprise her fingers shook whilst dialling. There was a tremble in her voice. Sudden new tears

125

pressed and threatened to fall as she fumbled her way towards contact.

"Is that the Alzheimer's Society?" she said, "I have someone...there is someone...I've told someone I would contact you...to help them with their wife."

Chapter Eight:

Elora and Lyse
The Fire

Elora wiped her steaming glasses on the mud free end of her cotton kerchief and squinted up the walkway. It was hard to see in this light and from this distance whether the shed door belonging to Lyse was propped open with the bottom end of her yard broom.

Behind her she sensed, rather than saw Barry Island's scowl. He was stacking that blessed bonfire again. It was already high enough. Where did it all come from? What was in that green petrol can? Elora sighed feeling defeated by his constant smoke attacks. She had hoped for a cup of tea and a little respite with Lyse. In winter, particularly, it was hard just to watch the heather and the remaining Brussels grow and remain oblivious to the malevolence scalding her back. It was a committee from the Dark Ages, full of prehistoric males locked inside their own misogynist retro minds.

Elora smiled, pleased with her rather literary hyperbole. Lyse would love that phrase and it would make a good cartoon. When she got home she would draw an enormous bonfire with easily identifiable caricatures dancing round the flames like the schoolboys from Lord of the Flies! That would make her feel a lot better. That and a huge, no, an enormous glass of the left over cheap white wine Rae had left behind after their last and, as it turned out, final row.

Elora suspected that Barry's scowl had intensified as she heard the slosh of something liquid. Immediately her nostrils were assailed with the sharp sickly smell of paraffin followed by an unnecessary overloud rattle of a match box. She glanced down towards the Stores. Prosser and friends would slouch up any minute now to join the party.

Smiler had taken to humming "If you can't stand the heat get out of the kitchen." It was infuriating but still it went against the grain to retreat and go home but ... Elora hesitated. She peered hopefully up towards Lyse's shed which did seem to be open after all. With a practised movement she rearranged her face into a disinterested pose and gripped both arms of the wheel barrow, pausing only to hoist her manure shovel on board.

Lyse met her midway with her own barrow and shovel. So far it had been an unusually dry and mild February. The raised beds had been easy to clear and the manure would be light to shift, especially with a younger pair of muscles to help.

"Hi girl friend," Elora called, "Ready to shovel some shit, whilst they shovel their shit?"

Lyse tossed her a spare pair of thick rubber gloves, "You bet, kid. Let's get shovelling!"

An hour had passed and Elora had hardly given a passing thought to what was happening down the far end of the Site. She hefted the final load over the wooden sides of the last bed and watched Lyse expertly rake the muck until it covered even the corners. Perhaps she should give in and agree to share this large space as Lyse had suggested more than once.

As she walked down to the shed to turn on their new, jointly owned, gas cylinder stove for tea she looked about her. The plots to her left and right were well dug and cared for but somehow seemed more inviting and less restrained. Weeds were definitely allowed and there were carefully placed bonfire bins like Lyse's own, set on concrete slabs close to water and sand. It was like being somewhere else entirely. Even the birds seemed to sing braver, louder and longer. The stray cats felt free to lounge on the grass or stroll into the sheds on a chilly day like today. Elora crossed to the shelf and shook out some biscuits for the skinny old tortoiseshell with the torn ear stretched out as if by right, on Lyse's grandma's old armchair.

As the kettle began to sing Elora took out two fold up chairs and a table and set them up just in front of the steps where they could have a clear view into the school playing fields and down into the beginnings of the older part of the village. She deliberately kept her back to her far off plot not wanting to spoil her restored mood. Although she could smell the occasional faint waft of wood smoke and hear the fainter crackle of a fire beginning to burn she did not notice the mushroom cloud of grey black smoke that had suddenly appeared behind her shed. Nor did she see the great dirty flakes of burning ash wafting into the air and then dropping onto anything in their way.

Lyse was still at the high end of the patch replacing her tools. From there she had a clear view of the entire allotment. At first she shrugged at the rapidly expanding smoke cloud but then frowned at the bright luminous flames of yellow and reddish orange which were dancing and swirling in every direction. Suddenly, from the heart of the bonfire a long spiral of white flame leapt to a great height. Only moments later an enormous explosion rattled every greenhouse window pane causing the roosting birds to take flight in squawking protest. Its echo and the snarl and bite of a fire out of control reverberated and continually repeated throughout the quiet village, accompanied by muffled yells and expletives of confused alarm.

From her vantage point Lyse watched in horrified surprise as the next explosion blew the bonfire apart and hot ribbons of fire began to fall like flaming snow onto one wood or straw pile after another and then began snaking their way up the paper thin walls and roofs of ill made sheds. Finally, she began to run down to where Elora stood, steaming kettle in hand, as if rooted to the spot.

"What the hell?" Lyse gasped, pushing the chairs apart and striding up the steps in search of her mobile phone. "What did they have in that fire to make it do this?

"I expect that was the tank of my motorbike. I had just filled her up," Elora said her voice vague and distant as she continued to stare in stupefied fascination at the unstoppable progress of the blazing inferno, "It's a good job that was only my second best bike and not the classic Triumph 500 Dad left me, or I'd be proper annoyed."

***

An hour later, Elora, now shaken from her stupor waited patiently until the fire brigade had left and then marched up to the circle of woebegone soot smudged and smoke blackened men. She trained Lyse's torch from one to the other and then onto the shadowy remains of her shed, possessions and bike.

"Well, I hope you're satisfied!" she said coolly as they squinted and shuffled and turned away from the accusing beam. "What did the fire chief call what just happened?" she demanded of them.

In the silence that followed Prosser coughed a smoky cough and muttered something incomprehensible to the stony faced Smiler who was busy calculating the loss of his own shed and all his winter crops.

Barry Island kicked out at a blackened wood panel that had belonged to his cold frame of precious early seedlings and growled at his friends, "Don't blame me. Blame that girl and her bloody motorbike."

Elora turned to Lyse and said loudly, "What did the Chief call it Lyse? Maybe you know as they won't answer me?"

Lyse who had been busy using her flash to photograph the cordoned off and incriminating wreckage took a quick shot of the guilty arsonists and then shoved her phone back into her jacket.

"Negligent arson Elora." She answered calmly and clearly into the still smoking near- night, " Neg .. li ... gent arson!" As if an apparent afterthought she added, "I just love Facebook, don't you?"

"Yeah!" yelled Elora over her shoulder, "See you in court bitches!"

The two women linked arms and turned as one hurrying their way to the gate which was still just visible in the rapidly fading dusk. For a while they were quiet, their busy minds still processing the enormity and the repercussions of what they had just witnessed.

"Why don't you come home with me Elora?" Lyse said finally, "I can drive you back later after I've made us some dinner."

There was a long pause. Elora was tired. What she needed was a strong drink and somewhere to cry and rave at will. Lyse would not mind the crying or raving but did she...

As if reading her thoughts, Lyse gave her arm a friendly squeeze and said quickly, "I'm not much of a drinker as you know but we do pass the Spa and they sell alcohol all hours."

"Can we have ice cream too?" said Elora, "but all my money went up in flames along with Henry."
Lyse experienced a swift pang of alarm, "Henry! That's not your stray is it, or your robin?"

"Henry was my second best bike." Elora explained with a small sad smile. "There was a tenner in the saddle bag."

"That's alright then," breathed Lyse, "Oh god, what am I saying? Poor Henry."

"Poor tenner!" Elora said with the beginnings of a near hysterical laugh, "Poor Barry Island! Poor Prosser! Poor Old Smiler!"

They grinned at each other under the street lights. "Who's *not* smiling now?" said Lyse.

Elora began to hum a familiar refrain which turned into a loud and laughing duet all the way down and into the Spa:

"If you can't stand the heat get out of the kitchen!"

**

Lyse

Lyse had stumbled from her bed to feed the insistent George, dragging jeans and a t- shirt with her, deciding to use the shower room down stairs rather than wake her guest. She had a slight headache. There was a ping followed by a sharper stab every so often behind her right ear. She winced at the kettle's shrill whistle and hurried to turn it off, filling the teapot clumsily before taking down the two largest mugs in the cupboard. She grimaced in self disgust as she considered the variety of empty bottles and used glasses untidily spilling over into the sink from the draining board. Wine, the bottle of beer she always kept in for her friend Betty and the half bottle of Bristol Cream she had bought to take up to her mother's next week. How much of it had *she* actually had?

She frowned. A hazy recollection of her agreeing to just sip at a glass to keep Elora company swam to the surface. That was all or was it? Another flashback of the night before pushed its way through the insistent hammering inside her head. Three glasses in a row: "We like this one. We like that one. Ooh we don't like that one!" and "But we'll drink it anyway."

Lyse went to the sink and poured a large glass of water throwing it down in one long gulp. She was parched. Her throat felt raw, her tongue, swollen and furry, scrapped unpleasantly at the roof of her mouth. Her lips were dry and this headache was sending her blind. This must be a hangover then... and if she had drunk all she imagined then...then what else? Had they...had they really? Yes really.

Lyse was conscious of a slow blush and a heat rising at the back of her neck. She had a glimpse of long dark hair spread across her pillow, a heart shaped face smiling up at her. A pair of deep brown eyes bereft of those over large glasses, somehow made vulnerable and irresistible. Soft lips pressing and coaxing her own, long silky limbs and ... abruptly she turned her attention back to the tea tray. Perhaps Elora preferred coffee, not tea in the morning. If so, did she take sugar? She placed the miniature glass vase of snow drops in the centre but then self consciously replaced it with the sugar bowl. Had she really just...just...with someone whose morning drink preferences she didn't even know?

Lyse lifted the tray and then paused. Were the covers heaped high on the other side of the bed been Elora or had she slipped into the spare room sometime in the early hours? Had she already left and taken the long walk home to feed her cats before going to work? Slowly she replaced the tray and sat down at the table and willed her memory to function with some vestige of clarity.

They had kissed in the hallway. It had begun as a warm, drunken, very friendly kiss goodnight but had somehow continued into her bedroom and then the warmth of the alcohol and the mutual fondness of their friendship and the heat of the day's events had lit up some kind of fire of its own. They had tangled themselves together laughing and breathless and, because it was Elora their love making became ever more loud, enthusiastic and somewhat experimental, lasting until the first pale light of dawn. And then, inexplicably they had both drawn away from the other. What had been said to break the spell? What had she said in response? What had she said to make Elora look so suddenly crestfallen, so shy and uncertain?

"OMG!" Elora had exclaimed her face flushed and grinning with delight. "That was mad...just wonderful and mad...and I've loved you for ages. Can we be together?"
Lyse saw herself frantically rolling off the bed and pulling on a shirt that may not have been her own, saw her arms tightly folding protectively around her body, saw the decisive shake of her head and heard again the crass, hurtful thing she had replied,

"No Elora. I'm sorry. We can't. It's mad alright but not wonderful. It's all wrong, you and me. I want us to be the way we were" she had begun to gabble, begun to cry, "Not this. Forgive me I'm just far too old, far too set in my ways, far too..."

"Lyse don't say that. You're not old." Elora rushed on anxiously, her words tumbling into each other as she struggled to express herself. "Well maybe you *are* a bit old but my Dad always said that age is just a number on a birth certificate. Surely you think that? You *must* think that."

Lyse had felt her hands begin to tremble with the beginnings of a panic attack and also a sickening rise of nausea which had had her fleeing to the bathroom.

Now as Lyse sat listlessly sifting sugar with a spoon in and out of the bowl she decided that it was the comment about age and birth certificates more than the unaccustomed amount of alcohol in her blood stream that had made her sick to her stomach. It was not so much a hangover but another long suppressed memory that was causing this persistently aching head. She had heard similar words once before. Had believed, had hoped with a mad, wistful impossible hope. An image of another younger woman, this one tall and over slender, with ear length blond hair and light, blue grey eyes ghosted from the far forgotten corners of her mind. She heard again that deep low seductive almost whisper, "Come on Lyse. Age is only a number on a piece of paper," and shuddered as fragments of later words, quick spite filled words laced with venom pierced her heart afresh.

Lyse dropped the spoon and from long unconscious habit deliberately squashed every fragment and thought back into oblivion. After a few more minutes she resolutely picked up the tray. She took her time with the stairs, trying to work out what she could say to Elora. How could she keep their friendship without having to try and explain a complicated and distant personal history? One she had only just managed to piece together which was still blurry, troubled and long, long ago.

Her bedroom was empty after all, the mound no more than a crush of sheets and a duvet. She crossed the landing and gave a tentative knock. After a pause and another half hearted rap she carefully opened the door. The bed still fresh with clean untouched linen stared reproachfully back at her. Lyse, half relieved but stricken and disheartened carried the tray back to her room thinking to try the tea anyway although expecting it to be stewed and cold.

As she had thought, the tea came from the pot cool, dark brown and unappetising. Instead she remade the bed and picked up her clothes which were embarrassingly spread throughout the room and carried them to the bathroom to hide in the wash basket. She shifted her bundle into one arm and fumbled for the light switch. This was her one windowless room and it was only once the light above the sink flickered on that she found the note on her mirror. In the pink lipstick Elora always favoured was a large crooked heart and inside a flowing script with the message:

"We will always have bonfire night."

End of Part Two

Part Three

2018-2019

"..don't be, don't be afraid...Our mistakes were bound to be made...But I promise you I'll keep you safe." Sleeping at Last 2015

Chapter One:

Dian

Dian is persuaded as far as the bathroom door before she sees the tall woman in the white plastic apron and cap holding out a large white towel in her long arms. She grips the door jam with both hands, plants her feet firmly apart, digging her fingers into the wood with all the apparent strength of Hercules.

This bird one with the white...this white...brings... cold... sharp hurts...NO!

The tall, narrow old fashioned bathroom is all white tiles, white fixtures and fittings, a far off white ceiling. Dian's disjointed recall dimly recognises the sound within, the falling, the splintering and the rushing of...*what*? She clutches harder. She can hear it gushing into...*what*? An invisible fearsome something.

This one with white wings brings...the drop...the ditch...the ice spits...NO!

Dian gives a backward kick as William tries ineffectually to prise one hand from the door. ***"Cunt!"*** she yells. William steps away, fearful of *that* word from his wife's mouth rather than her angry foot. He looks across at the woman, Jeannette, and turns his own lips down apologetically.

"Don't worry Mr Wilson, I've heard worse," she reassures and takes a tentative step forward hiding her frustration: if only the walk in shower had been organised ages ago, too late now. "Come on in Dian. It won't take long. You'll get cold if you stay there." Jeannette takes another small step and then another until they are just an arms- length away. She smiles down at Dian and tries to hold the wild darting eyes with her own. Carefully she gentles one finger and then another from the frame until one hand is in her own. With the other she flaps opens the towel wanting to cover the shivering woman clad only in a thin nightdress.

At that moment the door bell rings and repeats upstairs. Gratefully William mutters something and limps away.

Those women have arrived early, the woman from Bluebird late. Good. He hurries to let them in. Now they'll see what he has to cope with. Perhaps then they won't be in such a hurry to judge and make unhelpful telephone calls that subject him to prying visits he has not asked for.

From somewhere deep inside the careening kaleidoscope of her mind's eye Dian no longer sees the woman's kind arm and warm smile but rather the wide, heavy sweep of swan feathers, at the same time she hears fragments of a poem and then a fleeting image of an ugly statue, the nape of a woman's neck in a cruel beak. A sudden resurge of latent memory hurtles with a vivid picture of Dian the child running and screaming from the beating of huge white wings, the hissing and snapping of swans at her heels: a park, a pond, a ditch and a drop. ***NO!***

Get off...away with your indifferent beak...And Agamemnon dead! She cries out and continues to yell, pulling her hand away, snapping at the woman with bared teeth until she lets go.

Dian's terror follows William down the stairs and through the open door. For half a heart beat Lyse and Erica stare at each other aghast before Lyse pushes past William and rushes up the stairs, almost falling in her panic. Jeannette is surprised to see not William returned but a smallish woman with close cropped salt-and- pepper hair dressed in youthful jeans and a T-shirt.

"Go to her bedroom and find a dressing gown," Jeannette says calmly. Their eyes meet across the struggling terrified figure. "If you can't find one get a dark towel from the linen cupboard, as dark as possible."

Lyse nods and turns to scramble up the three remaining steps and into the bedroom. Inside she reaches for the kimono hanging from a hook, hesitates. How long since she has seen Dian wear this? Those familiar colours of burnished red and gold, the gorgeous dragon, the tail curling from its sleeves, the soft feel of a silken sash she had untied during their long nights together. How can this have happened to that seductive sleepy eyed woman who had so often sat across their breakfast table clad only in this beautiful thing?

No...No...white...indifferent beak...leave me...leave me...!

Lyse pushes aside the kimono and the quick pain of memory and drags a dark thick towelling gown from off the crowded hook. She pulls open the linen cupboard and throws its contents onto the floor until she finds a large navy blue beach towel. She carries these to Jeannette. Between them they eventually encourage Dian into clothes of a sort. Lyse wipes the hot tear stained face with a damp cloth and asks

"What happened?" she questions diffidently, feeling strangely humbled by her ignorance, "Is this a new thing?"

Jeannette sighs. How many more times can she bear to do this? Once again she patiently describes how people with Alzheimer's disease somehow, out of the blue, lose all perception of water. They can hear it, she says, they can feel it, but one day they just no longer see it. All they know is a threat, a sound and a feel that frightens and hurts. White merges into white and becomes a confusion of unrecognisable shapes. There can be hallucination, fragments of memory which cause more confusion, more panic.

"It's important," she says, "To remember it's the disease. Not the person."

Lyse hardly dare hear or ask more. She flinches away from knowing what it means. Jeannette wonders who this woman, who obviously loves her client is. She watches the way the woman now kneeling at Dian's feet is carefully putting on a sock and making her smile with a pulling of toes and a silly nursery rhyme. She considers whether she should speak first to the husband, who has chosen to hide somewhere downstairs, decides that there is something between these two that means she has a right to know, perhaps even as much right to know.

"Dian hasn't liked washing for quite a while," she continues gently with regret, "but until today I've usually been able to talk her into it. It looks as if the Alzheimer's is progressing down into the more severe stages."

***

143

Ruby and William

Ruby put down her scissors and checked her watch. It was past twelve. Whoever was knocking on her door was not the postman and unlikely to be Robert. He was in Sheffield.

The heavy knocking began again, paused and then repeated. Through the glazed glass door panel she could just make out the tall outline of a man. She took off her reading glasses and squinted. It looked like William. Surely not though? He never turned up without warning. He was proper like that. Anyway, he was increasingly tied to the times the carers could take his place with Dian.

As she stepped nearer the outline became clear. The tall stooping figure was unmistakably William. She frowned and shoved her glasses into the apron pocket. Involuntarily she glanced at the hall mirror. Why had she cancelled her hair appointment? If only she had bothered to give it a good brush this morning. Relieved that she had, at least, resisted the urge to keep on her cosy old housecoat and slippers she smoothed down her jumper and twisted at her skirt before hurrying the last few steps to the door.

"Why William, this is a nice surprise," she said her smile of welcome slipping a little as she looked up into his pale strained face.

William had not meant to call on Ruby. He had a long list of calls to make. Although none of them were as pressing as the desire to get out of the house and away from that strange half demented woman. Now he was here he had no idea what to say. His car seemed to have turned onto her road as if on autopilot. He attempted a small self derisory joke.

"I've run away," he said with a crooked faltering smile, "Well, only for now, I suppose.

Ruby looked down at the step, half expecting to see a suitcase at his feet. This was definitely William but not the one she knew. He was usually such a manly man, self contained and not given to emotions or jokes. Her hazel eyes widened in concern as his bottom lip appeared to quiver and what might be the start of tears stood on his eyelashes.

"Come on in." she said, taking hold of his sleeve and guiding him through to the kitchen, "Whatever is the matter, my dear man?"

"Am I a dear man?" he asked in a low tone, as if to himself, "Am I really a dear man or a bad man?"

"Whatever do you mean William?" Ruby growing uneasy, exclaimed, "Of course you are a dear man, a dear, dear man, the dearest and most decent man I know," adding with a note of finality, "everyone thinks so. Everyone knows so."

Alarmed at having betrayed her secret feelings so baldly, she turned away and busied herself with switching on the kettle and organising the tea things, giving them both a moment. William mollified but not convinced picked up the photo album Ruby had been updating and studied the smiling family pictures. How lovely the much younger Ruby was, untidily plump and glowing, holding hands with her grinning stocky husband. A boy in short trousers and a girl with messy hair ribbons were half hiding behind their parents, the boy pulling a grotesque face, the girl frowning at him. He turned the pages slowly with a growing envy and a deep sadness he had never acknowledged before.

He thought of the few photographs he and Dian had. Just a few black and white copies of their wedding, older sepia toned ones of their parents. There had never seemed much point in taking photographs or keeping albums. Here was a wonderful document. It was a testament to a happy family life lived in glorious Technicolor.

"Perhaps if we'd had children things would be different now." He muttered in the same subdued tone as before. "We couldn't seem to have any. It may have been my fault or Dian's. We never did find out why."

Ruby pushed a cup of tea across to William and picked up her own, "I wouldn't want to be without them, certainly," she said but privately thinking that they were often a mixed blessing, especially Robert and especially now as he grew older and more like his father every day. There were times when he wearied her with his opinions and pompous over bearing ways.

Although he had never actually said so she was sure that he would not like to see her and William at the kitchen table together but here they were anyway. And something was badly wrong with William and she wanted to help him. She would sit with him and she would help him.

For a while they fell into their usual easy companionable silence, her quiet presence, the rather overloud clock tick, the occasional chink of a spoon were all oddly comforting to William. Ruby resumed her pasting and printing of names and dates into the album. William silently, abstractedly, ate his cake and drank his tea, his hangdog head drooping and dejected as he stared vacantly at the table cloth.

Finally, he looked up and across at Ruby and realised that more than anything he wanted to keep the good opinion of this unassuming homely and kind hearted woman. It was an opinion he had always taken for granted but now felt he no longer deserved.

"Ruby," he said girding himself for censure, "I must tell you that I haven't been a particularly good husband. Not always a nice man and hardly ever a dear one."

"Oh?" Ruby reached out a hand and squeezed his, "What's made you think these silly things, all of a sudden?"

William, his throat straining in his eagerness to confess, rambled on and on, listing every failure and oversight right up to his flight of that afternoon before finally he trailed off exhausted.

Ruby had listened attentively, although part of her mind was replaying her own difficult final ghastly months with Douglas. She remembered anger, impatience and guilt, the frequent desire to run away and never go back. She gestured to the pile of photographs and said suddenly all matter of fact,

"No one's marriage is ever all party picture postcards. Memories of the good times come later, I've found."

She stepped briskly to the kettle and refilled it, "It's time you let others help you for a change. You must stop pushing people away." she said simply, "and you can count on me, my dear, dear man."

***

Erica

It was past three in the morning. Erica could not sleep. It was always more difficult when Stephen was off on one of his overnight Friends of the Earth workshops. She sighed and pulled out the milk saucepan. These days it was hard to always feel quite as friendly towards the earth as she used to. She turned up the dial on the central heating. At least she could ratchet up the heat without a prolonged discussion on global warming.

Erica loved their home, its wind leaking windows that rattled in even the slightest storm, the awkward old fashioned plumbing, the battered and bruised stone quarry flooring that was a nightmare to keep clean. They had begun their proper married life here once they had decided on a family. It was big enough for their five children, their partners and all their grandchildren to stay together for any family occasion. True, Stephen didn't always like a full house. She did.

Stephen was talking about downsizing. First it was an electric car then solar panels and now a move into a much smaller eco friendly house. It was a wonder he hadn't suggested a Yurt and living off the grid completely.

Erica took her hot chocolate to the kitchen table and sat with her back to the radiator and deliberately pushed aside her irritation. Marriage was often all difference of opinion and then give and take. Fortunately theirs was a strong one. There was going to have to be a compromise somewhere and perhaps it should start with the car? She sighed and picked up another chocolate biscuit.

Dian and William's marriage was made of a far different metal. Her fatigued thoughts strayed back to the major reason for her wakefulness. It was hard to summon up much empathy for that man at the best of times but after today even she had not bothered to defend his behaviour to Lyse. Hadn't he literally run away? She had watched as he had rushed through the hall, flung open the front door and then drove away with a squeal of brakes, as if the hounds of hell were after him. And perhaps they should be!

It was now well past three forty five: those awful hours, she thought grimly, where grief always lives. Dian was such a loss: an incomprehensible living loss. Screwing up her courage to keep visiting when so much worse was to come would mean more than one sleepless night. Erica remembered the booklet in her bag that Lyse had pressed on her. That nice sensible woman, Jeannette, had left a depressing selection on the hall table that she had pretended not to notice.

"Knowing what to expect is half the battle I suppose," Lyse had said, diplomatic but very insistent. "Perhaps it's about time we informed ourselves rather than getting sideswiped every time."

As Erica mounted the stairs she lifted her bag from the banister uncomfortably aware that her predisposition for procrastination did often leave her taken by surprise. Dimly she recalled a sheaf of papers that she had preferred to let alone in her office drawer for far too long until Dian had prompted her. As Dian had said then, and she had been right,

"It's time to face the music and dance, my dear!"

Chapter Two:

Robert

The fridge was almost empty. The sandwich fillings, the ones kept especially for him, were not in the lunch boxes as usual. He looked at the big clock on the mantelpiece. Twenty five past twelve. No sandwich fillings and no Mum. That was twice this month. Twice he had called in and twice she was nowhere to be found, at least last time there had been something decent he could eat.

Robert opened the bread bin and took out a couple of slices and flung them into the toaster and then hunted for the Marmite, waiting impatiently for the kettle to boil. He sat down drumming his fingers on the table his dark heavy eyebrows knitting together, his lips twisting in disappointment. Where had she got to? He really needed to talk to her. He had promised Lisa. Now he would have to go home and admit that he had, once again, not discussed selling the house and finding something sensible like those sheltered housing blocks half her friends had already moved into. The place was looking a bit shabby and the garden was going to give problems sooner or later. He sighed, feeling suddenly

151

tired, wishing he could afford to cancel the rest of his appointments and go to the pub for a proper lunch.

The bread was not a bit fresh. What was going on with Mum? He went to push aside the bulky half finished photo album at his elbow but instead pulled it towards him leafing through its pages as he disconsolately munched at this toast. Most of the childhood snaps he barely remembered except the one of him in the garden with the parents and his twin, Lilly. How old had they been? He studied his child self and saw a fresh faced mischievous boy of about 12 in school uniform, socks at half mast, laces undone pulling faces at his sister. His gaze moved onto his parents. His mother looked much the same as now, younger of course but here was Dad as he used to be, his shirt sleeves rolled up, his navy tattoos blue inked across his muscular forearms, stocky and sturdy, seemingly invincible.

A sudden sense of loss crept across his mind as he wrestled with the slow changes life had brought along with it. His Dad dead these five years; his sister living in Australia, he was nearly fifty and his Mum...what was going on with his Mum? He took his plate and mug across to the sink glancing at the time. From the corner of his eye he saw the sharp edges of what appeared to be a card, or something like it, propped behind the clock, almost as if in hiding.

Curious he pulled it out. It was a large birthday card entitled "To a Special Friend." Inside he read the rather formal inscription from William Wilson before placing it carefully on the table. His mind leapt back to the afternoon of the Tea Dance and the man in the car waiting outside for his mother. He remembered the way their heads had bent towards each other in familiar greeting.

As he picked up his bag and jacket he considered replacing the card but left it where it was. So, if that was what is going on with Mum and this William Wilson, this married man, it was time she knew what he thought about it because he did not like it: did not like it at all.

***

Ruby

Ruby breathed a deep sigh of relief as she caught sight of Robert's car turning away from the junction of Welcome Avenue. Robert, like his Dad, did not approve of wasteful taxis. She wondered why her son seemed to be taking on the mantel of all the more unlovable characteristics of his father as he grew older. Could it be helped? Was it in his DNA? He would have definitely questioned the amount of shopping she had brought home too: just like Douglas.

Later, as she considered the unwashed cup and plate of burnt crusts on the drainer she felt only a little compunction at having forgotten again to stock up on his sandwich fillings. Surely his wife could pack a lunch box for him along with the children's? What was going on with Robert? All that Douglas-like drumming of fingers and the knitting of brows meant he was working himself up to saying something. Whatever it was she was bound not to like it. Her mind sifted through the possibilities and her eyes took in the shabby paintwork of the kitchen diner, its faded and cracked linoleum. Through the window she could see the tall grass and the weedy flower beds, the shed door half off its hinges. She would have to call in Care and Repair before he started talking about sheltered housing.

Ruby brushed aside all thoughts of repairs and the prickly subject of moving house keen to get started on the freeze and reheat menu she had decided to prepare for William and Dian. Carefully she unpacked the final bag, checking its contents, putting to one side the pre-chopped packets of fruit and nuts along with the mini cartons of blackcurrant and apple juice that Jeannette had suggested would help prevent Dian from getting dehydrated.

Humming absently, Ruby lifted the photo album thinking to take it to the safety of the sideboard. Upon catching sight of her precious card, face down and pinned beneath their family photographs as if in searing filial condemnation, Ruby took a quick step away. A small sound of surprise and hurt disappointment escaped from the back of her throat as she clasped the book against her chest.

For a long moment she stood as if winded, her face flushing and then draining of colour, hurt and disappointment evaporating into a growing flood of burning indignation. How dare her own son come into her house and spy on her, to pass judgement on her actions without knowing what they were or why. Ruby, with an exasperated sigh, snatched up the card and replaced it behind the clock. Methodically she began to work on the vegetables, finding an odd kind of furious solace in chopping, dicing and slicing until every item was practically desiccated.

As she worked Ruby thought not of Robert or of William but of the shrunken white haired figure she had been visiting almost every day for the past month. Invariably she would find her seated or rather slumped in the corner of the sofa, sadly and very obviously now incontinent. She was invariably clad in a soiled and shabby outdoor coat, once worn with such enviable panache and style. Apart from the bright blue eyes that would momentarily meet hers or a fleeting glimpse of that old infectious grin there appeared to be nothing more than a mocking ghastly semblance of the living breathing woman that had been Dian Wilson.

Ruby knelt awkwardly to light the gas oven holding on to a chair back with a shaky hand. It probably was time to switch to a nice modern electric stove at least. Once upright, she unconsciously straightened her shoulders, lifted her chin and pressed her lips together in a firm line. Of course she liked William, she had always liked him and yes, she had grown to think of him as a dear friend. Often she had, she conceded, dismissed Dian as merely a woman careless of her great good fortune.

As she went on with her food preparations Ruby diligently scrolled down her many memories of Dian, the bazaars and uproarious bingo calling nights, the countless crockery they had washed and dried together in that old cracked enamel sink, the decades of after school clubs and hectic outings to Barry Island and beyond. Finally Ruby acknowledged that Dian had always been a friend to her: and a good one, at that.

By the time Ruby had everything safely in the oven and the freezer bags at the ready, she had promised herself, that no matter how late in the day she was going to be a good friend to Dian. If Robert, or anyone else for that matter, had anything to say about it, then they had better watch out!

Chapter Three:

Lyse

As Lyse finished raking up their rows of potatoes she reflected that Elora moving onto the plot was working out well. It was a lot more fun too. Elora's way of selecting potato varieties was an eye opener: Charlotte's as "Charlotte Bronte was a great writer." Vivaldi - his music is "sublime"; King Edwards because, "at heart I'm a traditionalist." The choices were also, for sensible horticultural reasons sound. So they were both happy. And what if she did occasionally catch a speculative twinkle in Elora's eye? It was easy just to pretend not to notice.

It was one of those beautiful late April very early mornings when everything was beginning to blossom or bud and the sun already stood high in a cloudless and vibrant blue sky. Elliot was such a pessimistic dope to call it the "cruellest month." Perhaps she was mad to have arrived for the dawn chorus but the crescendo of birdsong was always overwhelmingly moving. Next time she would try and identify the thrush from the blackbird, the chaffinch from the wren or the robin. That intention was always forgotten though.

An old memory flitted into her mind, seeming to come from nowhere. Dian and she had often awoken in the still half dark to the strains of the Gregorian Chants filtering down from their ceiling which was also the upstairs flat. That too had been overwhelming and moving and in their early days had often led to sleepy lovemaking. Lyse shook her head from side to side, as if brushing away an annoying fly or wasp, not wanting to spoil her mood for a change: wanting to delay an inevitable drop back down into that morbid chasm of loss she was unable to shift for long.

Even so, as she left the neat lines and walked down to the shed her mind became busy with Dian again. In particular, who was this Ruby woman? She was too old to be a Bluebird carer and William had not thought to explain her presence, had not even introduced her, leaving that to Ruby herself. Whoever she was Dian always greeted her with a grin and a semblance of her old infectious laugh. Perhaps that was all that mattered. Perhaps she should get over herself and accept her changed status as merely an old friend?

The bleep of a text alert broke into her thoughts. Glad of the distraction, she pulled out her phone and found it was from Cassie. Lyse grinned, it was still all in capitals. Should she put it out of its misery and show Cassie how to use upper and lower case and the auto correct? Cassie resented using mobiles, and only ever did as a last resort, so maybe not.

Lyse flung herself down into the grubby but roomy armchair, once a prized possession of her grandmother's and unfolded her pocket glasses, painstakingly divining the meaning behind all the misspellings. Next time she would return the first call left on her answer phone and not duck and dive. Cassie never gave up so why fight it? Elora, that's why. Lyse always had the uncomfortable feeling that Cassie had more than a little second sight or was it just an overdeveloped intuition? Either way, Elora was not something she wanted Cassie to quiz her about because if she did, she would get it out of her.

GOT FREE AFTERNON. MARGi POND PLANTS FOR UR NEW POND. WILL CYCLE DOWN AN MEET YOU AT ALLOTMT IF YOU LICK. SEE YOU ABT 12.30?

So, a bribe and one Cassie knew she could not resist! Their pond was in desperate need of more plants and Cassie was the pond expert. Elora would be disappointed if she refused them and well, Elora was not coming up until this evening, so...

Ok. I'm just popping home for breakfast. I'll make us some lunch. See you later.

***

Cassie

Cassie bumped her way down the allotment path and thankfully pulled up outside the shed door still propped open by an old yard broom. It had been a harder and longer cycle than she had remembered. Cassie eyed the rusted screws of the hanging top hinge and considered whether Lyse even had such a thing as a screwdriver amongst the clutter of tools that seemed to have doubled alarmingly since her last visit. Did she really need two of everything? Lyse was surprisingly unhandy when it came to minor repairs. Would the offer to fix the door offend? Perhaps she really did prefer the odd brick or broom handle.

Lyse was nowhere to be seen although her car was parked at the far end, the boot open. As it swung shut a familiar cropped head popped up and a gloved hand waved in greeting. Cassie propped her bike on its stand and hurriedly began to liberate the box of plants from its elastic ties rather than give in to the ridiculous urge to rush over and give Lyse a big hug. Or better still a smacking great kiss. As she slowly straightened, trying not to spill the overflow of water and plants she covertly appraised the diminutive figure sauntering towards her with her own box of the promised snacks. Apart from the inexplicably scalped and now naturally white hair Lyse had hardly changed in the twenty years they had known each other. She had kept her compact sporty figure and was somehow more attractive than ever. Why had they spent so many years doing that silly moth to a flame dance? If they waited much longer it would be too late. Why was Lyse playing so hard to get when the two of them together made such sense?

"Hello!" Lyse quickened her pace, realising, as she always did when confronted with Cassie in the flesh, how beguiling she had remained regardless of the passing decades. Who else could look so good in Lycra cycle gear in their mid sixties? Even that incongruous helmet with the flashlight taped on top gave her slightly squared jawed profile the look of an endearing mischievous puck-like figure. But did this perpetual mutual spark of ... what...something... really mean that they could make any sense as a couple?

With awkward self- awareness the two women bumped boxes and kissed cheeks, their eyes held just a fraction longer than necessary both pairs seeming to ask the same question.

"Let's have a look at these beauties," said Cassie, unwilling to ask just yet. She purposefully made her way across to the fledgling pond all business on the outside yet inwardly determined to find the kind of steely resolve it would take to ask. Ask she would, come what may.

***

Whilst Lyse was out collecting their order from the Tai takeaway Cassie had worked her magic on Lyse's long well scrubbed wooden table by throwing over a large rainbow coloured cloth she "just happened to have in her saddle bag." Keeping a careful eye on the wall clock she gathered every tea light she could find then lit and arranged them artfully throughout the room, switching off the overhead light, leaving only the heavily shaded standing lamp in the far corner.

Plates and various other containers warming on a low oven Cassie rifled through the mixed assortment of knives and forks flung carelessly in a drawer, finally selecting those with the yellowing ivory handles with Sheffield steel stamped on the back. Lyse's nostalgia with her family's left behind fixtures and fittings was rather sweet she supposed but it would not hurt to have at least one decent dinner service, cups that matched the saucers, some wine glasses as well as tumblers and cutlery that did not hark back to the days of Imperial plundering of countries and elephants!

"Dinner ho!" Lyse yelled pushing open the door with a foot, both hands full of steaming bags.

The unexpected enchantment of the scene caught her mid stride, ridiculous tears welling in her eyes as she surveyed the Aladdin's Cave that had once been her comfortable but merely functional kitchen.

"Oh, Cassie, this is... It's lovely," she breathed, her eyes taking in the myriad of tea lights that flickered and danced; their reflections merging into the failing light with the falling purple of dusk beyond. The balmy spring air was still warm through the half open French doors and the blackbird began to sing as if on cue. Before she could think better of it Lyse dropped the bags and hurried the few steps to where Cassie stood smiling across at her polishing one of her grandma's old spoons and said, "Well, if you are trying to seduce me this just might work."

Cassie carefully set down the spoon and placed both hands around the waist of this paradox of a woman she had wanted and waited for until almost into old age. "I certainly hope so," she said kissing her lightly on the lips, "but as we've left it this late in the day, let's eat. I've brought the wine. We'll both need a bit of Dutch courage tonight, don't you think?"

Lyse shook her head decisively. "I really do hate the taste of alcohol, it's ginger beer o'clock for me." Reaching up to kiss Cassie in return she added, "I love the taste of you though."

Cassie tightened her hold on Lyse and looked down into those dark blue eyes from her four inch advantage. For the first time she was sure there were no signs to misread or wrong signals to trip her up.

"You know what?" she said, not wanting to let the moment pass her by yet again, "Let's put the dinner on hold and keep the wine where it is for now."

***

Cassie and Lyse

Lyse woke first, the soft regular breath of her companion announcing that she still slept. It was already mid morning. Cassie's hand rested warm across her thigh. Lyse studied the face in repose, noted the lashes thick and curled, the skin lightly wrinkled at the eyes and mouth but smooth, youthful and slightly tanned from working outdoors in all weathers. Did they make sense together? Their lovemaking had certainly told her they did.

She relaxed back into her pillow and allowed herself the luxury of recall, right from the first tentative shy and exploratory caress, then the deepening endless kisses that had built into a fierce slow burn of an unstoppable passion she had thought long forgotten. All those wonderful, wonderful mutual climaxes until they had fallen suddenly asleep mid-kiss, mid-caress. Was this possible? Could she move past not just Dian but also those ancient buried wounds she was only just beginning to bring to the surface? Would Cassie....

Cassie's eyes fluttered open, as if even in sleep, she had sensed the danger in the growing agitated thoughts of the woman by her side. Her lips widened into a delighted smile as she gloried in the sight of her new lover and in her continued state of undress.

"It's too early for thinking," she said, her voice thick and sleepily drowsy, "but," she added moving her hand down a little and inching closer for a kiss "but not too early for lurve."

Lyse, eager for the kiss, shamelessly, joyfully aware of the heat and damp already between her thighs, circled Cassie's neck and pulled her close. "You are so right Cassie King" she said with a long satisfied sigh," It will never be too early or too late for that."

"I know," murmured Cassie into her neck, "and we still haven't got round to the dinner or wine."

Chapter Four:

Lyse and Erica
Singing for the Brain

"What's happened to your mini sports?" Lyse stood a few feet away and critically observed the rather ugly box shaped vehicle Erica was clambering out of. "Is this a courtesy car or something..." she trailed off realising her amusement was patently obvious and unappreciated.

"I traded it in for this," Erica replied sharply beginning to rummage through a large eco string bag dangling from her wrist, adding with an exasperated grunt, "It's electric and its name is Compromise."

"Well," Lyse just could not help the laugh, "That shade of purple is certainly eye catching...won't be difficult to find in a multi story car park." she said. "That's got to be some kind of consolation."

"Quite," said Erica reminding Lyse strongly of the days when a "Quite" from Erica during a meeting had always immediately quashed any unwarranted jocularity or flippant response.

"My turn to drive," said Lyse, smothering another laugh, turning smugly towards her new sleek black Hyundai i30.

The two women were preoccupied and silent for half the distance, enjoying the kind of comfortable silence that only very regular travel companions could achieve. Finally Erica looked up from the leaflet she had been perusing and said,

"How do you think this Singing for the Brain is going to work out?"

Lyse raised her eyebrows and pursed her lips. This had definitely not been her idea of a bearable afternoon with Dian. She had begun to appreciate Ruby Winters always being on hand allowing William to escape upstairs to look at his emails or whatever it was he did up there. A whole afternoon in close company with him would be difficult and she would be robbed of her few precious moments of aloneness with Dian.

"I've been reading those leaflets you gave me," Erica persisted, realising that Lyse was unable or unwilling to respond. "Music and song is linked to the side of the brain that hasn't forgotten," she intoned straight from the brochure in her hand, "rhythm is preserved along with melody and emotion."

Lyse kept her gaze firmly on the road ahead and managed no more than a strangled word or two and a reluctant nod. Is this what hoisted by your own petard meant? How many more jolly jaunts would there be in future? Too bad that Ruby and Erica seemed to have bonded over the tea and sandwich making. She and William had shared a brief but meaningful look of ill disguised reluctance, for once on the same side. He could hardly say no as it was being held in his own community hall could he? And well, she was far too cowardly to face Erica's disappointment, or worse, her disapproval.

***

Dian

The passing sweet fragrance of lilac prompts Dian to inhale deeply, as if long deprived of oxygen. For a blessed moment her mind stalls in its chaos and confusion. Natural light and sound seep into her consciousness bringing quiet and calm. Her fingers grip the steel arms of the wheelchair but she knows this one and forgets to be afraid.

This wheels brings a happy...brings outside...takes away empty...

Half way across the road Dian cocks her head at a shrill sound. Suddenly she is all ears and eyes her attention captured by the boy on the bicycle as he ferociously rings his bell and flies past. Her gaze is drawn downhill until he is gone. When they reach the pavement and bump up the kerb she gives a sharp amused chuckle.

Upside... downside... she says quite distinctly.

A front door opens just as they begin to navigate from the chair and into the car.

"Hello Mr Wilson, Mrs Wilson," says the old lady with the pretty dog that Dian often watches from her window. His wet nose nuzzles into Dian's outstretched palm and they whimper their pleasure.

***

William

"Put some music on William love," said Ruby flanked by Lyse and Erica in the back seats "Get us all in the mood for a good old sing song."

William fumbled with the radio dial and threw her a grateful look through the rear view mirror. Was he the only one to find all of them crammed together on their way to a Singing for the Brain session excruciating? A little grimly he returned her reassuring smile, wishing the afternoon over and done with. He resolved to try his best, to be the kind of good sport he had never been able to be for Dian. Perhaps Ruby would notice, even though his wife would not, maybe that Lyse, his unshakeable nemesis if ever there was one, might bring herself to give him a little credit where credit was due. He would sing if it killed him – and singing always did – he could never manage more than a whisper, not even in church.

***

Lyse

Throughout the short journey Lyse sat silent staring straight ahead with a small polite smile plastered to her lips. Dian had only been able to manage a few shaky steps into the hall before collapsing into the wheelchair Ruby had deftly assembled. How had that happened without her noticing? Why had someone else thought about providing one first? How long since Dian had met them at the front door or left her chair to greet them? Why had those few simple words at the kerb come across as remarkable and unexpected?

It was as if in the blink of an eye more of her Dian, her precious Dian, had disappeared. She had been completely preoccupied by her own heady nose-dive into a romance with Cassie. Lyse slunk further down into her seat, chill waves of her old habitual senseless guilt settling heavy, oppressively on her chest. Dian's head, with its familiar patch of un-brushed hair on the back, was only a reach away from her hand. With an effort she resisted the urge to smooth it down as she so often had in their shared past. Instead she gripped at her knees and ignored the itch. Dian's hair was the very first thing she had noticed on the day they had met. She had hardly been able to wait until she could get home and scribble down a fragment of a poem in her diary.

***

Lyse remembers
Diary entry

We have a new boss! And I have to put my foot in it straight away! Oh pants and crap!

She in a bright blue dress stood
in the doorway a flash
of pure white and silver in
dark hair.
Her crimson lipstick
lips pleasantly framing
a question.
I cracked a casual joke but must confess
that as the door closed on her
ironic lift of a well plucked eyebrow
I was seriously smitten!

***

 Lyse studied that hair as it was now: unwashed, uncut, thin, oily, an ugly yellow tinge staining the white, obliterating the silver, the dark another lost memory.

As she unclipped her seat belt and hurried out to open the passenger door to help all her long held guilt metamorphosed into a permanent deep and bitter realisation. There was nothing she or anyone could do, not even science it seemed. And definitely not a Singing for the Brain session but...

But if for one brief afternoon, Dian was given back a little memory and a little happiness she would endure anything, even "William love" and the mysterious Ruby Winters. Lyse quashed all those self conscious stomach cringing thoughts of having to sing silly songs in public and took charge of the wheelchair.

"Come on Ironside," she murmured into Dian's ear as they jostled their way through the narrow swing doors, "let's get this show on the road," and was rewarded with what she chose to think was a familiar eyebrow lift of amusement.

***

Erica

Erica, once settled looked about her with a teacher's curious expectant eye. Most of the group they had joined were from the local care home and were older than Dian, apart from the woman on the end seat. Was she even in her mid fifties? She was carefully, stylishly dressed, a silk scarf tied neatly at her neck, an expensive looking watch glinted beneath the cuff of her smart grey wool jacket. For a moment Erica thought she may be a volunteer or a relative until she noticed how stiffly upright she sat with her hands clasped tight and unmoving in her lap. Her face was fixed in a pose of restrained confused terror. The man next to her, eyes infinitely sad and downcast must be her husband. He seemed fixated with his own feet as if he dare not look around him and witness the living ghosts of what his wife would surely become.

What was behind all those vacant or confused looks that uncomfortably mirrored Dian's? Was it possible that their minds were just a blank chasm of nothing? How were these unlikely looking blokey blokes, one with a guitar slung over his shoulder in workman's boots and the other, bald with an earring going to capture their attention? She had a vague recollection of singing with her school choir to a large group of elderly inmates. With youthful ignorance she had wondered, just as she did now, if there was anything behind their vacuous thousand- mile stares.

To her surprise and relief the two did not immediately offer up a melody of dated and familiar songs they were expected to sing with any kind of real or simulated gusto. Instead, after Mikey the Milk had strummed a couple of over loud attention grabbing chords the bald one stooped down and picked up a battered looking cardboard covered book and took a pencil from behind his ear, introducing himself as Ricky from Rotherhithe and his book as a diary, dating back the fifty years to the day of his birth and written by his "dear old Dad."

***

Erica and Lyse

"Well," Lyse conceded as soon as they were safely off the slip road and onto the endless semi-clear stretch of motorway leading them homeward, "that was not what I expected."

Erica gave her skirt a surreptitious little tug over her knees, "I thought it was rather successful," she said trying not to sound too triumphant. It was hard though, as the whole experience had been far better than she had feared. The phrase exhilarating and uplifting with just a little poignancy and sadness in the mix fairly summed up the afternoon for her. The two men, incongruous and out of context as they may have appeared had certainly weaved a rather wonderful, incomprehensible magic.

"God bless those two men." She said and meant it, "Who would have imagined that kind of response?"

"They certainly played a blinder," Lyse agreed thinking of that first heartbreaking hesitant whisper Dian had uttered when asked her name and then of the way she had eventually been charmed into that impromptu ragged and rather raucous glee club of singers.

"Mind you, what's all this "William love and dear" from Ruby all about?"

Erica had also noticed the number of loves and dears, but deciding to take the practical view observed neutrally, "Isn't it great that she appears to have the time to help out so much?"

Lyse shrugged and for a while kept her focus entirely on the traffic as it began to slow and then crawl to a stop to make way for one and then another blur of yellow and white as ambulances, flashing lights and blaring horns, raced past.

"The wheelchair was a great help too." Lyse managed a belated admission as the vehicle in front lurched forward.

"Yes, so God bless Ruby and her late husband's wheelchair, I'd say."

"God bless is a bit beyond me Erica," Lyse said with an ironic smile, "but yes, dear or William love notwithstanding, yes."

"And this afternoon was a rare good afternoon was it not?"

Lyse gave a resigned shrug. Why was Erica always so doggedly positive? That unworthy thought hardly had time to settle before a sudden and more welcome picture materialised of Dian's eyes bright and alive and her rusty singing voice loud and defiant, her fists pumping the air.

"Did you see how Dian was making everyone laugh with the way she was stabbing her imaginary knife during that ridiculous, "Why, why, why Delilah?" she said with a delighted grin.

"Oh yes, so Dian like." Erica returned the smile, "She certainly hasn't lost her power to engage an audience. They were all stabbing by the second chorus even that rather stiff younger women sat on the end."

There was something about the style and dress of the woman Erica mentioned that had caught her eye too.

She must be about the same age as Dian was when she was first diagnosed. They had once managed a visit to the Dementia cafe but Dian had refused to return, stating adamantly, "They are not me. I am not there yet." That woman had most likely had similar thoughts, at least when she had first arrived.

Both women lapsed into their private thoughts allowing the motorway to eat up the remaining half hour of their unexpected good afternoon with Dian. Lyse with an unspoken wish and Erica with a similar heartfelt prayer. Please let there be more good afternoons. Let there be more music and more laughter and a bit more magic for Dian whilst there is still time.

***

Robert

At the sound of the car drawing up behind him Robert hurriedly withdrew the spare key from the door. He shoved it deep inside the pocket of his raincoat before dumping his briefcase on the top step. He then strode the few steps to the garden gate and roughly dragged it open.

Ruby winced as the hinges squealed a protest and its iron bottom scrapped along the cracked concrete of her path. She placed a staying hand on William's as he reached out to switch the ignition back on, "No need to hurry away dear," she said with determined composure, "it's time you were reintroduced to Robert anyway."

William studied the stocky and frowning middle aged man for a moment whilst the cooling engine ticked over and his courage failed him. Robert had been one of a handful of truculent teenage boys that had hung around on the edges of the youth club, always looking as he did now, his thick eyebrows creased together and his lips in a long sullen line. If there was ever a fight Robert was always in the thick of it.

As he reluctantly opened the car door and stiffly unfolded his long body onto the pavement he remembered that Dian had been the one those boys had warmed to. She would laugh off their scowls with a "Come on now, turn that frown upside down!" and then challenge them to a hotly fought darts match or a game of table football, which she invariably won. He wondered as he held out his hand in greeting how Robert would react if he were to say that now.
"How's your wife?" said Robert, his frown deepening as he squeezed the proffered hand a little too firmly, "not with you tonight?"

"Now Robert, you know Mrs Wilson is unwell these days." Ruby said mortified. How like Douglas at his most censorious he had become lately. "We've just had a lovely afternoon together at the community hall, a Singing for the ..."

"Shall I get Dad's wheelchair from the boot for you, Mum?" Robert dropped William's hand and walked to the back of the car. Without waiting for an answer he pulled awkwardly at the locked boot handle twice before stepping back, confused and embarrassed by that sudden irrational desire to wrest back his dead father's property from this man.

"Keep the wheelchair in the car for now William dear," Ruby looked coolly across at her son, and then apologetically at William, "It will help with the doctor's visit tomorrow."

William hesitated, "Thank you Ruby," he said eventually, "and you Robert. It will be a real help until I can get one of our own."

As he thankfully pulled away from the curb relieved Ruby had not invited him in, William saw Ruby place a gentle and placating arm through Robert's, handing him her bags, allowing him to walk her up the path to the door.

Just before he turned onto the main road he glanced through the rear view mirror catching a glimpse of the faded blue painted door as it closed behind mother and son. He felt unaccountably discomposed by the difficult encounter with Robert. The sooner he got a wheelchair the better.

A few minutes later, leaning heavily against the wall to support his suddenly tired and aching leg he fumbled in his pocket for keys his mind still groping for the reason behind Robert's obvious disapproval. With slow unaccustomed insight he discerned that maybe inside the man Robert, the truculent and insecure child still lurked: that the wheelchair was not the real issue. He had been quick to point out that he already had his own wife at home. Was *he* the real issue? Did Robert imagine that he might want to take his mother away from him, or at least his father's wife?

Later, William pushed aside his half eaten food, suddenly having no appetite for his undercooked ready meal. His thoughts continually returned to Robert. That comment about his wife waiting for him at home buzzed and stung at him like an angry wasp. He snatched up the remote and snapped at the red button, giving up on the television as well as his dinner. How many evenings alone like this one had he spent, before and after Dian's diagnosis? When had he ever had a wife waiting for him at home? Not in over forty years of marriage. What kind of life might he have lived if he had married someone like Ruby?

If Robert did think that he wished Ruby was his wife, was he so off the mark? Was he the only one who thought that?
Did Ruby think it? Did he?

***

Dian

That evening Jeannette is pleased to find Dian unusually compliant and good natured. Humming in a strained and gravelly tone throughout the hated bedtime process she allows a cursory strip wash and a complete change into a nightdress even consenting to the removal of her shoes and socks. She balks at the tooth brush though and again it is left for another day.

A happy...sing, sing, sing! She smiles at a residue of memory a stabbing in the air and the joyousness of laughter.

Bird one shut cloths...night then. She searches through the sticky tangle of her wounded brain for anything else left of the afternoon of **happy** until she finds what she is looking for.

Night, night, night Delia! She calls down the stairs to Jeanette who is making her way to the kitchen.

Night, night, night Delia she calls again at the sound of the front door closing as William prepares to drive Ruby home.

Night, night, night, man or winter or bird...someone, anyway... she mutters before drifting off to sleep, still humming.

Chapter Five:

Lyse and Cassie

Lyse washed up with only half her mind on the task at hand. Through the window there was the pleasing sight of her lover bending over the remaining outdoor tomato plants with the watering can. Cassie was always so ready to get outside. Any stray job would do as an excuse. She had already replaced the broken pane in the greenhouse and fixed the garden gate. They had only got home a couple of hours ago. Lyse took a moment to admire the back of her neck and her bare shoulders tanned to a light coffee coloured brown. She let her gaze linger on the firm muscled calves also tanned beneath her impossibly youthful cycle shorts. Cassie straightened, picked up the stiff yard broom for a final sweep round and waved blowing a kiss with her free gloved hand.

Although now three months into their love affair- Lyse still refused to call it relationship – her heart did that silly somersault and her pulse quickened at thoughts of the night to come. She ran the final plate under the cold running tap and placed it in the drainer debating whether she should bring out a couple of cold drinks.

Perhaps they could snatch a quiet moment watching the sunset which was bound to be glorious this mild mid September evening. Lyse also debated whether to risk spoiling their tranquillity by suggesting again that Cassie came with her to visit Dian.

On the one occasion she had mentioned the possibility Cassie had leaned abruptly away on the back legs of her chair as if suddenly confronted by a particularly disagreeable image or a bad smell.

"No. No I don't think so." She had shaken her head very decisively, picked up her glass and drained it quickly adding with a hint of apology, "I'm nowhere near as brave as you. I prefer to remember Dian as she was, it's easier."

Lyse remembered having bit back a retort, "Easier for whom? Not me, not Dian." She had turned away instead and busied herself with feeding the surprised and gratified George for a second time that evening.

Now, as she lifted down the wine glass and the tumbler she indulged in a brief bitter moment of contemplation. Who had bothered to stay in touch? What had happened to that Old Flame, for example? The one who had rung Dian up early one morning and put the spoilers on their idyllic love affair? He had soon disappeared back into the ether when the news of Alzheimer's had filtered down to him. Not just him either. Perhaps they all found it "easier"?

By the time Lyse had poured the drinks and was half way up the garden Cassie was already lazily sprawled on a canvas sailor's berth they had picked up in an old boatyard in Cornwall. "Why don't you put those down," she suggested with a sly smile and an exaggerated pout on her lips, "Come and join me. There's room enough for two."

Behind the trees that fringed her boundary the sun was beginning its golden graceful retreat. There was the familiar sweet song of the blackbird and the grumbling roosting caws of rooks as they settled. The night scented stock and the late summer roses faintly perfumed the air. A few bats wheeled and circled, searching for insects. The natural cycle of life and love could be so beautiful but so brutal and so brief. She studied the gorgeous scantily clad woman still smiling her invitation from the precarious swing seat tied between shed and a sturdy hawthorn. They were far too old to frolic in a garden hammock, surely?

"Carpe diem?" Cassie suggested and held out a hand.

"My thoughts exactly," said Lyse. She smothered her doubts and clambered awkwardly in to join her.

"Well, now you've finally taken the plunge," said Cassie, "how about a kiss?"

Lyse snuggled up to Cassie's warm well defined and work hardened body and sighed, "I don't mind if I do." she said, pressing her lips on Cassie's. Deliberately she parked the certainty that difficult times and difficult conversations were bound to come. She closed her eyes, ignored the insistent ring from the telephone with a final hazy thought "but not tonight. Tonight is just for us, for now."

***

The persistent blink from the far corner of the kitchen reminded Lyse that she had heard the telephone ringing once or twice before it was silenced last night. She had taken very little persuasion to ignore it when they had eventually come in from the garden. Looking across to where it sat, inconceivably and precariously balanced on the window sills edge, she was loath to dispel her languid state of satiated calm. Gradually though its scarlet flicker impinged itself on her conscience and so she eventually crossed the room, poised her finger above the Play button but hesitated once more.

The whine of her elderly pipes and the erratic stop start of water from a faulty shower head began in her downstairs utility room. There would be plenty of time to listen to the messages before Cassie was finished. For someone who always flung her old work clothes back on from the day before it was surprising how long Cassie spent in the shower. She always smelt delicious though, woody and earthy but somehow clean and fresh.

She hit Play and waited expectant. Mum, Sal, Keith which one was it to be? The voice was partly masked by the thick drone of static from her ancient machine. She would find time to replace it...soon. It was male and familiar but definitely not Keith. She moved nearer and cocked her ear towards the speaker. The voice and the drone continued. Was he talking to her or to someone else? She tuned to high. There was definitely someone else in the background. That voice sounded soft persuasive and female. A conversation then and not a phone message, the kind of thing her grandparents had often left for her mother to find and work out. Lyse smiled at the memory and pressed Replay as the message abruptly cut off supposing that If she could identify who they were then she might figure out what they wanted.

What am I supposed to say then...just ask her to give you a call dear...**I don't see why though**...because it wouldn't be very nice if she found out some other way love...

Lyse stabbed at Replay and listened again carefully: love and dear? Ruby's incomprehensible signature words for William. A chill of unease swept through her as she pieced together the other phrases ...ask her to call ...it wouldn't be very nice if...

The red alert continued to flash, reminding Lyse there was a second message. Uneasy she stabbed at the Play button taking a nervous step back as if whatever was to come from the microphone might bite her.

William Wilson here. Dian has had another fall and...

What fall? Another fall – how many falls? Why had she not known? Why had she not been told?

Lyse, took a deep breath and tried to calm down. They had been on holiday. It was her fault. She had not phoned. Her eyes filled with tears. Not even once in three weeks. Dian had fallen and what else, what else had happened whilst she was off having fun with...with... another woman? She pressed Replay.

Dian has had another fall and...what with the incontinence and...everything...well social services and so do I think she should go into nursing care. So she's going soon. I thought you should know.

Cassie stood uncertain between the alcove adjoining hall and kitchen watching her lover, her own alarm growing every time Lyse shook the black box and compulsively pressed Replay yet again. Finally Cassie quietly laid the broken shower head on the table and came up from behind, gently wresting the machine from her grip and guiding her into the nearest chair.

"Darling?" Cassie scrutinised the ashen face. "What's happened?"

For a moment Lyse just stared up at her, as if she had forgotten her presence, "It's a mistake. It must be." She gestured at the answer phone. "They are going to put her away."

"May I?" Cassie crossed to the dresser and pressed the button. The speaker was still tuned to high. Its begrudging and stark message blasted out and resonated off the walls for moments after it had clicked off. Secretly relieved to find it was not Margaret that was to be "put away" as Lyse had called it Cassie slowly digested the gravity of its content.

"I'm going to make us breakfast," she said decisively. "We won't talk about this until you've had something to eat and drink."

When Lyse merely shrugged and continued to stare down at her hands, her lips pressed together Cassie quickly crossed to the sink, filling the silence with the noisy reassuring gurgle of water into the kettle, the turning on of the gas, the collecting together of cups plates and cutlery: her heart sinking all the while. Her mind frantically searched for whatever it was she should say now that she had been ambushed by William Wilson and his crass message. Was it any wonder that Lyse could not stand the man?

"At least drink your tea Lyse," Cassie slid the mug forward. "Why don't you give Erica a ring?" she added with an uncomfortable awareness that, as usual, she was trying to pass the problem on.

"I think I will." Lyse said giving Cassie a sharp perceptive look before picking up the tea and hiding her eyes beneath the rim.

An awkward silence began to grow between them. A decent, loving person would offer to stay Cassie knew, they would not be sitting here like me, feeling trapped and cornered.

"I could stay until this afternoon, if you like," she was sure that her voice did not carry with it much conviction and so glancing across at the shower head she had put aside earlier she continued, "I've got the new part and my tools in my pannier why don't I fix that and then make you something for later?"

"It's up to you," Lyse said stiffly, scraping her chair away from the table and turning to reach up for the address book. "I want to print off my information on Assisted Living before I go down to put a stop to this madness. I bet Social Services didn't bother to give him that option."

"Lyse sweetheart, I know you feel you must still be involved in everything about Dian, but if..."

"Must be?" Lyse cut in, flushing and turning back to face Cassie, "Of course I must be. Do you think I'm a till Alzheimer's do us part kind of person? If William doesn't want her anymore than she can come here."

"That's a bit extreme isn't it?" Cassie stared at Lyse, "You can't mean that and besides the best place might be in a decent care home. It's not your decision to make, surely you realise that?"

"Yes, I do mean it" said Lyse, her tone hardening, "and yes it is. I should never have let her go back to him in the first place. I've always wanted her here. It's where she should be. I'm going to get her back."

"That's never going to happen, surely you can see that?" Cassie said frustration and a sudden stabbing threat of impending loss prompting her to rush on regardless, "and if by some fluke it did what would happen to our future, the one we could have together if only you would stop living in the past?"

"So, that's what you want me to do is it?" Lyse rubbed furiously at her eyes and glared at Cassie with something that seemed to her akin to dislike, "I am to forget Dian because she has no future? I'm to stand back and let him dump her into one of those awful places for the living dead?"

"They aren't all like that and it's not what I meant..."

"This has happened because I *have been* having my future when I should have kept her safe." Lyse said her voice rising. "Instead I've been running around the country with...with..."

"With me, you mean?" Cassie leapt up indignant. "That's crazy. Going on a holiday with me has made all this happen?" As the teapot and her elbow came into contact Cassie muttered "Shit" and stepped backwards trying vainly to stop its fall with a desperate hand.

Both women watched helpless as Lyse's precious teapot clattered onto the stone floor spout first and began to haemorrhage sticky orange contents from its wound.

"Shit!" repeated Cassie. She stooped quickly to pick up the pieces and to stop its flow, her face flaming with embarrassment. Why that teapot? Lyse was bound to turn it into some kind of ghastly metaphor.

"Well, for a first quarrel," she said as she carefully placed the broken pot into the sink and eyed Lyse warily, "that was a right humdinger!"

For a second Lyse forget the reason for the upset and gave a quick amused laugh, picturing again the consternation on Cassie's face as the teapot had spiralled down and crashed to its end at her feet. Instantly the laugh died in the back of her throat as she began to feel keenly its loss. Another piece of Dian she was never going to get back.

Suddenly exhausted and impatient for Cassie to leave so that she could get on with the real fight on her hands Lyse shrugged, "It was an accident. Why don't you get off? I'll clean up."

Cassie moved a step or two towards Lyse before faltering to a stop.

"If you're sure then" she said awkwardly, belatedly realising that feeling trapped and cornered was far preferable to how she felt now: excluded and superfluous. If Lyse were to give even a hint of a wish for her company she would stay and gladly. But it was obvious that Lyse had already begun to disconnect, her eyes were distant, her mind plainly back in the past with Dian. Their present and any shared future forgotten.

As she cycled late to the job Cassie sensed that her legs were frantically labouring up hill at an unnecessary gut busting pace. Although she tried to slow, her body stubbornly refused to comply. As her tyres ate away at the tarmac she had a growing conviction that with every yard and minute and mile the distance they were creating was not just from the messy tangle of this morning's argument but inexorably, inevitably, away from the woman she loved beyond all things. Was this why she could never make a relationship stick then? Was Lyse right to imply that she was the kind of person that was only" till Alzheimer's" do us
part?

***

As Lyse stood next to the printer, impatiently waiting for the final pages, Cassie's departure had already slipped from her consciousness. Her mind was frantically bullet pointing and listing possible outcomes in a confused rush of ideas and options. Once the printer juddered to a halt she swiftly made her way to the conservatory and sat in front of her A4 notebook and began to scribble down her ideas in untidy capitals:

- WM AGREES TO 24/7 CARE.
- HOW MUCH CAN I CONTRIBUTE TO THE COST?

At this second point she paused. Dian had offered her money once, a ridiculous amount; money in the tens of thousands. If she had taken it then she could have used it for just such a circumstance as this. Why had Dian wanted her to have it? Why had she refused?

***

Lyse Remembers

Lyse drove deliberately below the speed limit, ignoring the impatient gestures of the driver in her rear view mirror. Dian was gripping the stabilising handle above her head and from the corner of her eye Lyse could see that she was trying hard not to wince at each turn of the hill. These hairpin bends were hell with Dian in the car. There was the tell-tale flush on her high cheekbones, always a sure sign that she was experiencing those strange sudden anxiety attacks whenever a car was in motion.

As they finally reached the reassuring wide flat stretch of road they exchanged a mutually relieved and amused look before Dian tentatively released her grip. The man behind ostentatiously roared past with a finger wagging gesture. Dian waved gaily back and stuck out her tongue.

"That was rude of you Mrs Wilson," Lyse said grinning.

"Well darlink I cen alway blame the Alzheimer." Dian replied, adopting her favourite persona and giving her thigh a suggestive squeeze.

Lyse replaced the wandering hand back into Dian's lap, "Steady on old girl. If we crash I can't blame that on the Alzheimer." She said, grateful they could still joke together, even if it was about the ghastly spectre awaiting in their attic.

As they pulled into the pub car park and Lyse made to open the door Dian laid a restraining hand on her arm, "Just a minute kid," she said, pulling out a dog eared cheque book from her handbag, "I want you to help me with this. I can write the words but not the numbers. Isn't that odd?"

Lyse raised her eyebrows, "I don't mind but can't William help you pay the bills?"

"Not this one," Dian handed her the book and then hunted through her bag for a pen, "Write the numbers for me Sweetie and check the words just in case."

Lyse flattened the book on her knees scanning the half completed cheque. She frowned and glanced at Dian in surprise before fishing in her pocket for her glasses and slowly scrutinized each word.

"No. That's ridiculous," she said, touched but somehow also oddly offended, "I don't want your money. I've never wanted it and I certainly don't want it now. You don't need to start paying me just because, just because..."

"Oh don't *you be ridiculous!*" Dian snapped, "That's not why. It's my money and I want you to have it. I've given you money before and you've never been so squeamish!"

"But this is thirty thousand pounds." Lyse shook her head vigorously but then added hopeful "unless you meant to write three hundred that is."

Dian took hold of Lyse's hand and kissed it, then leant across and kissed her hard on the lips, uncaring for once of passersby, "I'm not gah gah yet! This is your inheritance. Early."

Lyse grabbed Dian's handbag and shoved the cheque book inside, shutting it away with a decisive snap.

"Leave it to me in your Will then" she said, "does William know you want to give me this?"

"No it's mine money...I mean my. If you don't get it... have it now all be lost." Dian saw her words running away from her and raised her voice to a frantic yell hoping to bring them back. *" Attorney gives him everything... he gets power everything... too late will come... everything!"*

Lyse and Dian had sat for a long long while, way past their table reservation time: Dian insisting in ever shrinking and confused half sentences and Lyse doggedly refusing until they finally trailed off spent and defeated.

As Lyse locked up and followed Dian's dejected figure into the restaurant area she sighed deeply, wishing she could agree, even just to take the cheque and leave it in some separate account. But somehow she could not bring herself. She contemplated William's reaction and imagined lurid newspaper headlines where she would figure as the artful lesbian who had tricked a fortune from a vulnerable, demented woman.

"I'm sorry my dearest love," she thought, "Too late has already come."

***

Lyse picked up the pen and wrote a rash of bullets, her mind tipping into overdrive.

- DIAN LIVES WITH ME – POWER OF ATTORNEY – he gets everything?
- HOW MUCH TO CONVERT DOWNSTAIRS?
- CARE – Bluebird. Social Services. Money?

As she reread her list, adding and subtracting, finding more and more questions and fewer and fewer answers a slow dawn of realisation took hold. Cassie was right. William was never going to agree. Legally she was out in the cold, invisible and voiceless.

Dian had tried to give her the one thing she had left to give: an inheritance for *her* future now that *theirs* was lost. Lyse pushed aside her pen and ripped off the list from the pad, screwing it into a tight ball, throwing it to the far corners of the room. She pressed her head onto the table no longer attempting to stop the tears leaking from her eyes or the chill feeling of helplessness seeping through every pore of her skin and into her heart, her blood, her bones.

What Dian had struggled to tell her was also true: ***"power... attorney... everything... too late will come."***

When the telephone began to ring she was tempted to walk away from its insistent demands and let it go to answer phone until she remembered the havoc caused by its last message. She picked up the receiver at a run and answered with a short questioning "Yes?"

There was a brief uncertain pause before a vaguely familiar female voice asked

"Am I speaking to Lyse? Is that you, Lyse dear?"

Angrily Lyse pulled her head away from the ear piece. Dear? Ruby Winters?

"Yes Ruby. How can I help you?" Lyse replied gracelessly. She and William would get no "dears" and "loves" from her.

There was a small cough from the other end, a slight anxious clearing of the throat, "Lyse dear, I'm so glad to be able to speak to you."

Lyse remained perversely silent, all good manners deserting her in a resurgence of her earlier fury.
Another small cough, the clearing of the throat, "Lyse love, I know William left you a very awkward message last night. He meant to have just asked you to call back but, well, really it's such a difficult time for him and..."

Lyse took a deep breath but still forgot to school herself into politeness. "He's not the only one it's difficult for Ruby," she said and added with a terse follow on "It's not an easy time for Dian *ever* is it?"

"No dear and not for you either." Ruby's unexpected reply, the kindness in her tone and her bravery in the face of rudeness from an almost stranger stopped Lyse in her tracks.

"No, it's not," she acknowledged her voice breaking, "I think just for once, William could have been a bit more considerate. He might not think my feelings matter but..."

"Of course they matter dear. Come down tomorrow afternoon and ask your friend Erica if you like. I'll make us all a big tea and we can have a nice talk about it."

No sooner had she replaced the handset than it rang again. This time she was careful to read the caller ID. Erica. She might have known.

"Erica love," she said sardonically, "I knew it would be you...dear."

Chapter Six:

Erica and Lyse

Erica took little pleasure in the brightness of the early morning or the passing of ever increasing swathes of wildflower hedgerows; only in so far as they heralded nearing the end of her tedious journey. Why had Lyse deliberately buried herself in such an out of the way place? What was wrong with a well managed urban setting with everything no more than a walk, a bus ride or a short drive away? The countryside was all very well for the occasional weekend but for everyday living?

That satellite navigation thingy was not much help. Its imperious instructions only irritated, giving her no time to rehearse the kind of conciliatory logic that might convince Lyse to accept the reality they were now faced with. Impatiently she disconnected from the unseen "Janet" and tried to identify some of the suggested landmarks instead. There was the Co-op, the old bus shelter and at last, the left hand filter arrow on the traffic lights that led down to Lyse's small housing estate.

The front door was already open and Erica took a cautious step inside before calling out.

Lyse called back a fairly cheerful greeting which gave Erica heart. Perhaps this breakfast parley would go better than she had feared?

Lyse had taken a leaf from Cassie's book and had made the table welcoming, using the bone china plates, the matching rainbow egg cups and the genuine antique long handled egg spoons that Dian had given her. There was a tall tumbler with three very striking orange dahlias in the middle and looking very professional but out of place a moderately sized stack of computer printouts next to it.

From her carrier bag Erica pulled out her own slim collection of printed materials and placed them crossways on top of the pile.

"Oh!" said Lyse, impressed, "did Stephen print those off for you?"

"I'm quite capable of printing off my own documents I'll have you know," Erica replied rather tartly but with a small smile.

"Ah," Lyse smothered the urge to laugh and quickly moved on "coffee or too early for you?"

They both settled for eggs, toast and tea made in Lyse's second best teapot. They ate in a strained silence whilst their minds engaged in separate worries about the potential minefield of Ruby's "big tea." Lyse doubting she could keep her temper in check and Erica wondering just how rusty her once famed diplomatic skills had become with the joys of calm retirement.

Lyse filled the kettle for more tea and briskly cleared the table leaving everything, for once, unwashed in the sink whilst Erica diligently sorted through the paper trails, putting aside the "impossible" and "not an option" and keeping those she considered achievable.

Lyse set down the teapot and looked at the sadly reduced pile with more resignation than Erica had expected.

"It's alright Erica," she said with a shrug, "I've already worked out what's definitely not going to happen but what I want is to decide what we might be able to make happen."

The two women exchanged a knowing look. One they both recognised from the days when they had conspired together before presenting or defending their ideas to a potentially hostile audience to those Dian had often called "bigwigs" and Erica "kingpins." Lyse had, privately, very different, less respectful words for them as she now had for William. She had wisely kept them to herself of course and now decided that she had best do the same today.

***

The "big" tea
Dian

Dian sits at the table along with the others her dining chair the only one with arms. It is solid, substantial and necessary to keep her swaying slight frame from a fall. Her appetite at least, is still hearty. There are a variety of tempting finger foods placed on a napkin in easy reach. Jeanette discreetly guides hand to mouth and Dian opens her lips like an obligingly hungry baby bird. In between food Dian focuses exclusively on the handbag in her lap. The bag's zip her main preoccupation rather than the contents. Her stare switches from vacant to alert and then back to vacant drawn to an unseen horizon, rarely alighting on any of the occupants seated with her.

*Bird...shining...many...*Dian gives a bark of laughter as a memory momentarily slides back into place...*mad hatter...tea party...*

Lyse

Lyse, sat to the left of Erica and next to Dian safely ensconced between her and Jeanette. Immediately she began to struggle against the low gloom settling over her and could only toy with her plate of well filled sandwiches. The further drop in Dian's condition was inescapable and alarming. Any remnants of her impossible day dreams of a twenty four- seven care option had come crashing down after less than five minutes. Every extra minute added another extra layer of acceptance. She knew that William could have done many things differently or have done better for Dian, but he had done what he could, she reluctantly supposed. To leave her where she was for much longer was not safe, that was apparent. This part of her journey had come to its end. It was clear that everyone around this table, including her husband, only wanted what was best for Dian.

Covertly she watched Ruby as she busied herself making sure everyone's plate was full and that tea or coffee was always at the ready. It was hard not to like Ruby or not to believe in her good intentions. She was so careful not to exclude Dian from her ministrations, adding a few more chopped pieces of fruit or carrots along with extra finger bite morsels occasionally murmuring a few words as if asking after her wishes. Lyse observed the extra solicitous attention William was also receiving from Ruby with only the merest hint of irritation. He never had to fill his cup or to reach for another sandwich even his wish to move on to the well buttered homemade scones was anticipated. How he must love this. But who wouldn't? The sudden sense that she was also being watched caused her to look up and to her surprise, the still bright light blue eyes of Dian seemed to briefly fix on her, lucid and aware. Dian's sideways glance switched to William and Ruby with what, Lyse was convinced was a definite ironic half lift of an eyebrow before her gaze turned inward and drifted away.

Jeanette had also intercepted the look and was certain it was one that only those with a strong connection, probably far more than a friendship, ever shared. So was this the reason for the tea party and the particular reason why she had been invited? The move into a nursing care home was regrettable but necessary and one Lyse would naturally want to resist. She considered William, who was as usual, seated as far from his wife as possible and stolidly eating and drinking whatever Ruby put in front of him, like a man who thought this was his due. Or perhaps not...as a man who was using food and drink as a defensive, protective manoeuvre? He must find it irksome witnessing the warmth still evident between his wife and someone else, perhaps especially so because it was another woman.

Jeanette wondered, not for the first time, why anyone could imagine that anything as awful as Alzheimer's disease could miraculously turn a cold and distant marriage into a warm and loving one. They were still the same people, after all. Dian's brief response, her momentary unspoken communication with Lyse and her detachment from William on a daily basis spoke volumes. Jeanette replaced her tea cup and mentally prepared herself for a potential confrontation between two people whose polite public exchanges had barely ever disguised their mutual antipathy.

William

William had not been so engaged with his meal as Jeanette had imagined. He had noticed that shared moment between his wife and Lyse. There had been many such moments and also the occasional ill guarded word from Dian as her natural discretion and inhibitions had eroded throughout the years of visits from her two friends. He glanced across at his stranger wife who was absorbed with zipping and unzipping that bag and making low rough sounds only she understood. She could be clear enough though whenever he tried to help. It was almost as if she preferred to wet or soil herself rather than to have him touch her. Lately she had refused to be lifted whenever she fell and had fought him with irate curses or a flurry of fists following up with that awful familiar sentence from their past: "Leave me. I don't want you!"

His indignation at his unwanted visitors, his resentment at the bitter thought of having to explain himself to that one in particular faded into a confusion of contrition and self justification. Those words had been all too familiar throughout their married life. He could not prevent the vivid recall that swept through his mind, although he took care to hide his brooding thoughts behind the final coffee dregs in his mug.

He had never forced her, no, not quite that, but he was not innocent of coercion either. He saw his dishonourable self refusing to move from the doorway of the spare bedroom. His insistent demands rang as an echo in his ears. He could almost see the way his face must have turned ugly and twisted in frustration. He remembered how he had often kicked out at furniture and once at the cat until she had finally acquiesced with those dreaded words: "Alright then, if you won't leave me, but I don't want you."

William unconsciously bowed his head and tried to blink away those vivid pictures now come back to haunt him. Of all the memories Dian had lost he knew with a searing shamed certainty that she had not forgotten those and never would. All his best efforts since the diagnosis could never change their failed marriage. Alzheimer's disease and his past actions meant that no matter how hard he tried he could no longer be of use to the woman whom he had always faithfully but inadequately loved. But was it too late to be a better man, a dear man?

William pushed aside his plate and carefully placed his mug on top and then almost shyly gave Ruby a self deprecating smile. Somehow she had helped him, was helping him to become a better man, a better husband, even this late in the day.

"Thank you for a wonderful tea Ruby and..." he said surprising himself by a sudden sincerity, "and thank you both and Jeanette for all you've done over the years to help."

It was probably his imagination but had Dian's attention, for the briefest of seconds, left the handbag and focussed on him, her eyes uncannily clear. And in them had he seen, could he have seen, a faint glimmer of approval before the inevitable drift had taken her?

***

Erica and Lyse

"Fancy coming in for yet another cup of tea?" suggested Lyse, "We can look through those brochures Jeanette gave us."

Erica checked her watch, searching her mind for Stephen's whereabouts at this time of day, "No more tea for me. I'm awash but I've got an hour."

The early evening was as bright and as mild as the morning had promised and both women sank thankfully onto the wooden bench, glad to be out of the stifling heat of the car and into the fragrant open air amongst Lyse's well tended herbaceous borders. The hammock still swung invitingly from between its posts and Lyse deliberately turned her back to it a faint colour rising at the nape of her neck. With an effort she quashed all thoughts of Cassie and the dozens of unanswered calls and texts listed on her mobile, especially the last one: a bald **"SO IVE BEN DUMPED BY NO TEXT THIN?"**

"Let's get going on this lot then," she said swiftly, dropping the pile between them.

For a while they studiously passed brochures and leaflets back and forth reading carefully, sometimes between the lines until they both began to feel more than a little jaded with all the mission statements, grandiose guarantees of "person centred care, dedicated walkabout sessions and full timetables of activities."

"Beware of brochures bearing Mission Statements," Lyse half joked reminding herself of the many such statements had they concocted together in their gloomy basement office in the past.

"This Ty o Cof nursing care is very promising though, don't you think?" Erica passed across the final booklet she had deliberately saved until last.

Lyse was still chagrined at how easily she had been swayed by Jeanette's conviction that a nursing environment – "a good person centred environment" – she had stressed - was the best outcome for Dian. Lyse had watched Dian carefully, hoping in vain for some sign that this momentous decision about the quality of the rest of her life was not completely passing her by. It seemed to her that during those few minutes she had pushed through and through all seven or was it the eight revolving doors of her grief whilst Dian had continued oblivious and to worry at nothing but the zip. At one point she had emptied the contents onto her lap. Jeanette had deftly helped and encouraged Dian to replace the items scarcely pausing in her distribution of brochures and recommendations.

Lyse thought back to the continued questioning looks that "**Bird**" as Dian called Jeanette had seemed to direct at her. She really did appear to have welcomed her constant queries and the occasional forthright challenge. Lyse had to concede that she seemed to have offered her a careful kind of unspoken empathy. As she sat in the safety of her own garden rather than around that not quite convivial tea table, she was certain that at least one person recognised the validity of her loss and the frustrated sense of helplessness she had carried with her since that awful day nearly seven long, agonising years ago. If William had not exactly included her in the initial decision he was at least agreeing to her being a part of this one. He had sat quietly, rather diffidently throughout the "big tea" she realised now and wondered whether they had finally come to some kind of, if not understanding, at the very least, a truce.

"I know nursing care is the right thing for Dian," she said slowly her heart dropping but resigned at this final inevitable loss. "Let's go and look at this Ty o Cof and perhaps that Ty Melin."

"I'll give William a call and ask him to arrange it then," Erica said with a pleased finality, adding with what she hoped was the clincher, "and Jeanette happened to mention that she's just been appointed as Supervisor at Ty o Cof for nursing care."

Lyse snapped her head up and stared at Erica, her eyes widening in disbelief.

"Oh?" was her strangled muted response, "are you sure. Are you definite?"

Erica nodded, "It is such good news isn't it? It's so much better than we could have hoped for."

"Then Dian must go there. I know she'll be safe there, don't you think so too? " said Lyse still half fearful she had misheard.

"Yes Lyse, I think we have every reason in the world to think so." Erica gently squeezed her friends' arm quickly dismissing the temptation to confess to an earlier rather more exclusive tea party at Ruby's with just herself and Jeanette as guests.

There were times, as Dian had often said, when a conscience was a luxury, "that one just can't always afford, my dear." Instead she brushed down her skirt and began to make a move, "Come on it's getting late. By the sound of it even the birds want to go to bed. Let's go in and make that call shall we?"

The two friends listened for a moment to the blackbird's evensong as it soared and pierced the waning orange and golden dusk. Lyse sighed deeply, the heavy load her shoulders had carried for so long, seeming to slip away with the falling sun.

A once familiar wide delighted grin began to transform her face: one that Erica had almost forgotten. "Yes" she said, her own voice rising with a mixture of sorrow and joy as she too stood, "Yes let's do that."

Epilogue

"Goodbye my Lover. Goodbye my Friend." James Blunt 2014

Robert and Ruby

The first thing Robert noticed as he walked through the hall was the return of the wheelchair. It now stood in its proper place in the alcove. He stopped for a moment and rested a hand on its folded arms.

"Hello Dad," he said, feeling ridiculously sentimental, "Welcome home."

He walked on and into the kitchen. His mother was nowhere to be seen but on the table waiting for him was a plate with mini sausage rolls, cold cuts and a salad bowl. His favourite mug was out on the tea tray and a jug of milk stood next to the already filled kettle.

Glancing through the window he could see Ruby hanging out her washing in the billowing October wind and rapped on the glass. She looked up smiled and mouthed "Five minutes." He snapped the switch on the kettle and turned to pick up a sausage roll whilst he waited. He went back to watching his mother with a fond contented smile. She was pegging out her sheets making sure they got a good blow, as she called it. Normal service was well and truly resumed he decided. Mrs Wilson was taken care of and Mr Wilson would not be monopolising so much of his mother's time from now on. Result!

He continued to look out into the garden and slowly realised that the shed door no longer hung at an angle. There was a smart shiny new metal hinge and a matching bolt. He scrutinised the shed with a puzzled frown forming between his eyebrows. Was that a new felt roof and a fresh coat of green paint too? The borders were dug and weeded and the grass cut like the old days when Dad was there to do it.

As the kettle boiled he turned his attention away from the garden, filled the tea pot and sat down pulling the plate towards him. Robert ate methodically and thoughtfully. The kitchen seemed brighter than usual and somehow less cramped. There was the gap where the old cooker had been but it was more than that. His eyes swept the room taking in for the first time the pale primrose yellow of the walls and then up at the brightness reflecting off the newly painted ceiling which was minus the old plaited wire from which had dangled a nondescript lampshade. Instead there was now a very handsome quartet of proper led kitchen lights. Lisa had pointed out something similar last weekend, calling them some silly name like a "kitchen island." Robert gave a sharp intake of breath. They had cost nearly a hundred pounds.

His eyes left the lights and fell instead to contemplating the flooring beneath his feet. The cracked and ancient linoleum of his childhood had been replaced by a pale wood shade of very modern laminate. There was also a colourful non slip runner under the sink similar to some other kind of carpet in the hall. When he had come in he had only noticed the wheelchair back where it should be. During that short walk down the hall his feet had been silently cushioned by a long matt- grey entrance runner. Was there a change of paper too? He craned his neck and stared through the door and over the banister. Unfamiliar pale grey regency stripes were also marching up the stairs and beyond.

Why was she doing up the place all of a sudden? Dad wouldn't like all these changes except for the tidied garden of course. He remembered the odd cross words his parents had exchanged whenever Mum had wanted to decorate: Dad deploring the upheaval and the cost. Mum decrying "the state of the place."

A slow flame of suspicion began in his mind. His frown deepened and his fingers tapped restlessly at the table, which he saw, was thankfully the same one they had always had. Mum was expecting not only a new cooker this afternoon but also a replacement fridge and she had spoken of getting rid of the twin tub she had always said was good enough. Or was it Dad who had said that?

What was going on with Mum now? It was almost as if she was setting up home again, taking a new broom to the place; feathering a cosy nest for two but this time not with Dad but with... Robert flung his down his fork, abruptly losing his appetite and fought the urge to run into the garden and demand an explanation or reassurance or...something anyway that would

211

convince him that his mother had not completely lost her head over William Wilson.

***

"Hello love," said Ruby dumping the empty laundry basket onto the drainer. She raked a hand through her unruly hair relieved to be out of the autumnal mini-gale. "Glad you've helped yourself and not waited for me. Don't forget the salad now Robert."

Robert grunted and pulled the bowl forward not appreciating his mother's fussing for a change. Ruby poured their tea and sat opposite her son. That tell tale Douglas frown was back. What was going on with him now?

"What do you think of the house makeover?" Ruby decided to grab the bull by the horns, "I've been thinking of getting it done for ever so long and now seemed like a really good time."

Robert swallowed his sausage roll for once wary of speaking his mind. "It's all very nice Mum very smart but it must have cost a pretty penny."

"Care and Repair only send reasonably priced people. I found a very capable young lady for the decorating and a nice man for the garden." Ruby sipped at her tea unperturbed, "I can afford it. Enough money was *not* spent on decorating over the years for me to splash out a bit now."

Robert sniffed, deciding not to mention the cost of the lights or to ask the price of the flooring and to definitely leave the cooker, fridge and proposed washing machine for another day.

"Any special reason that now is a good time?" he ventured instead and poured them both more tea trying for a casual enquiry tone.

Ruby looked across at her son those usually warm hazel eyes a little sharp.

"I want the place nice and cosy for my house guest," she said. "Next week Caroline is coming back to do the bedrooms and I'm changing that difficult old bath for a walk-in shower." She picked up a pile of leaflets that had sat unnoticed on a spare chair. "My grant has come through. I'll only have to pay a third. Have a look at these and tell me which one you think would be best."

Robert's mouth began to form a perfect circle of shock. His frown deepened. Speechless he held out a hand for the leaflets and glanced at them. His eyes widened at the astronomical prices even a third would cost yet that hardly registered.

"House guest?" he said a flush of outrage beginning to colour his face and neck. "Do you mean that Wilson fellow? That old man must be nearly eighty. How could you think of moving him into Dads' house?"

"This house is my house now Robert," Ruby said calmly and quickly prised the brochures from his fist before they were completely crushed. "Do you think older people are incapable of falling in love? I'm only seventy five and there's life in the old dog yet I'll have you know!"

Robert stared at his mother, his flush of outrage subsiding into more of a blush of confused embarrassment. They *were* too old, surely? "He's a married man," he amended lamely.

Ruby allowed the silence to lengthen, her annoyance gradually fading as she observed her son's hurt bewilderment. "Robert dear, how old fashioned you are." She gave his hand a quick pat, "I am very fond of William," she admitted, "but not so fond as to shack up with a married man. Neither of us would feel comfortable with that. So we are leaving things are they are for the time being."

Robert let out a breath, "Well," he mumbled, now grappling with his mother accusing him of being old fashioned and using the words "shack up, and "time-being."

"Then who..."

"It's your Aunt Edna dear." Poor Robert, he definitely was a chip off the old block, so easy to windup. With a glint of laughter now behind the hazel of her eyes she added, "She's moving down from Lancaster and is going to stay with me for a while. We're both on our own and it makes sense. Your sister is coming over for Christmas and the New Year too, so we'll have a full house."

Robert's big bulky shoulders slumped in relief. "Sorry Mum. I got that wrong didn't I?" he said with a weak semblance of a smile.

"Yes dear, you did." said his mother continuing with a note of unarguable finality "But I will be inviting William here for Christmas dinner and on any other occasion if it suits me."

For a brief moment mother and son regarded each other cautiously across the table. Robert felt his idea, his comfortable idea of his mother, shift and rock. Was this really who his Mum had been all along? And if so, why had he ever thought she needed him to take care of her future? She didn't need him. She was already doing a good job of it by herself.

"But I'll always need my best boy Robert." said Ruby as if she could read his thoughts: which of course she could.

**

Dian:
Ty o Cof – 2019
Today

Dian's rooms are light and airy. The blinds on her big picture window are always lifted in the morning so that she can see beyond her four walls. Sometimes she can capture and hold onto the image of the magnificent cherry tree just about to blossom and sometimes not. It's warm and the window is open a crack to allow in the morning air already alive with birdsong and the distant sounds of people and traffic.

Today Dian prefers to stay abed again and slips peacefully between sleep and a waking forgetfulness.

"This is nothing to worry about," Jeanette assures Lyse, "Dian will have more sleepy days now."

She carefully explains about fragmented nights and the difficulty Dian has distinguishing night from day. How tiring eating breakfast and personal hygiene can be.

Yet still Lyse worries and sits fidgeting in the corner arm chair and counts how many "sleepy days" Dian has had over the past few weeks: far more sleepy days than alert days. Lyse longs to walk into the large cheerful residents lounge and feel the sweet relief of finding Dian ensconced, queenly, feet up on the dais of her recliner chair. She watches a while as Dian sleeps on, dreaming perhaps, beneath the faint fluttering of her closed eye lids.

Restless Lyse gets up and somehow resists trying to wake Dian, if only for a moment, just to see those forget me not blue eyes briefly light up in recognition, to feel that faltering caress on her cheek, to hear her strange new gravelly voice murmur "***shining comes***." Instead she wanders the room, admires the fresh bouquet of flowers and wonders who brought them.

She turns her attention to the photographs and examines each in turn. Until now she has always avoided looking at the black and white wedding picture that sits on the dresser in a smart black stand- alone frame. Lyse steps up close and peers at the tall beaming young man in the elegant grey trousers and old fashioned top coat and then at the smaller waif like dark haired figure. Dian, a girl of nineteen, clad in white, their hands are clinging together. Dian must be saying something provocative or even a little smutty, judging by that familiar impish look on her face. Lyse replaces it and moves away even after all these years feeling a sharp pang of jealousy. With an effort she reminds herself that Dian had said they had "been happy at first." A disappointing marriage could happen to anyone as she well knew.

The second photograph, in colour had been fixed to the wall and was somewhat askew of centre. Ruby and Dian, both in their late middle age are feigning surprise and delight that their cake table is already sold out and bare of everything but the patterned plastic tablecloth and a few unused paper plates. Lyse straightens the frame feeling obscurely pleased. Until now, she had been unaware that Ruby and Dian shared a friendship history independent of William.

The final photograph is one she had unearthed a few weeks ago and framed herself. The pure white wood compliments the vibrant colour of the portrait of five women varying in age and height. All are dressed in bright summer clothes, all grinning broadly as if sharing a joke. Four are standing on the higher or lower steps of their old school building and the fifth, a much younger Lyse, blond, sunburned and in sandals, sits at Dian's feet. She sees now that her grin is a little self conscious. It was the day of her promotion and she was probably the butt of their kindly jests and playful pleasantries. As she turns away and walks across to the bed in the hopes that the faint movement under the covers might mean she is waking Lyse recalls how proud and pleased Dian had been that day.

Lyse takes Dian's hand and brings it to her lips. She thinks that perhaps Elora is not coming with her guitar after all and that maybe, with any luck, when she comes next time, Dian will not be having another "sleepy day." She whispers, "goodbye my lover, goodbye, my friend" and gives thanks to the god she cannot quite bring herself to believe in for everything this woman, now so frail and fragile has been to her: her teacher, her benefactor, her rock, her shoulder to cry on, her lover, her friend.

Just as she begins to turn away surprisingly strong fingers grip hers. Dian's lids twitch once or twice and then decidedly open. The startling blue eyes swim into focus and meet hers and then drift towards the shape in the doorway: Elora, long glossy dark hair loose, guitar slung over her shoulder, clad in the shortest of polka dot dresses and the longest of slim black boots.

*Ah...*says Dian in her strange raspy voice...**shining one**...**singing bird**...her gaze gravitates to the window where the blue of the sky and the brightness of the sun filters through the leaf green of the tree...***blue and yellow up high***...

The End